D1015739

Volume I: Into the Hollow Earth

BY ANSON MONTGOMERY

CHOOSE YOUR OWN ADVENTURE® THE GOLDEN PATH™
PUBLISHED BY

CHOOSECO®
WAITSFIELD, VERMONT

Cover Painting by Nancy Taplin
Illustrated by Suzanne Nugent
Cover Design by Dot Greene, Greene Dot Design
Book design by Kate Mueller and Stacey Boyd

CHOOSECO

For information regarding permission, write to:
P.O. Box 46
Waitsfield, Vermont 05673
www.cyoa.com

ISBN-10: 1-933390-81-6
ISBN-13: 978-1-933390-81-9

Published simultaneously in the United States and Canada

Printed in the United States

0 9 8 7 6 5 4 3 2 1

This book is dedicated to
Avery and Lila.

And to Ramsey.

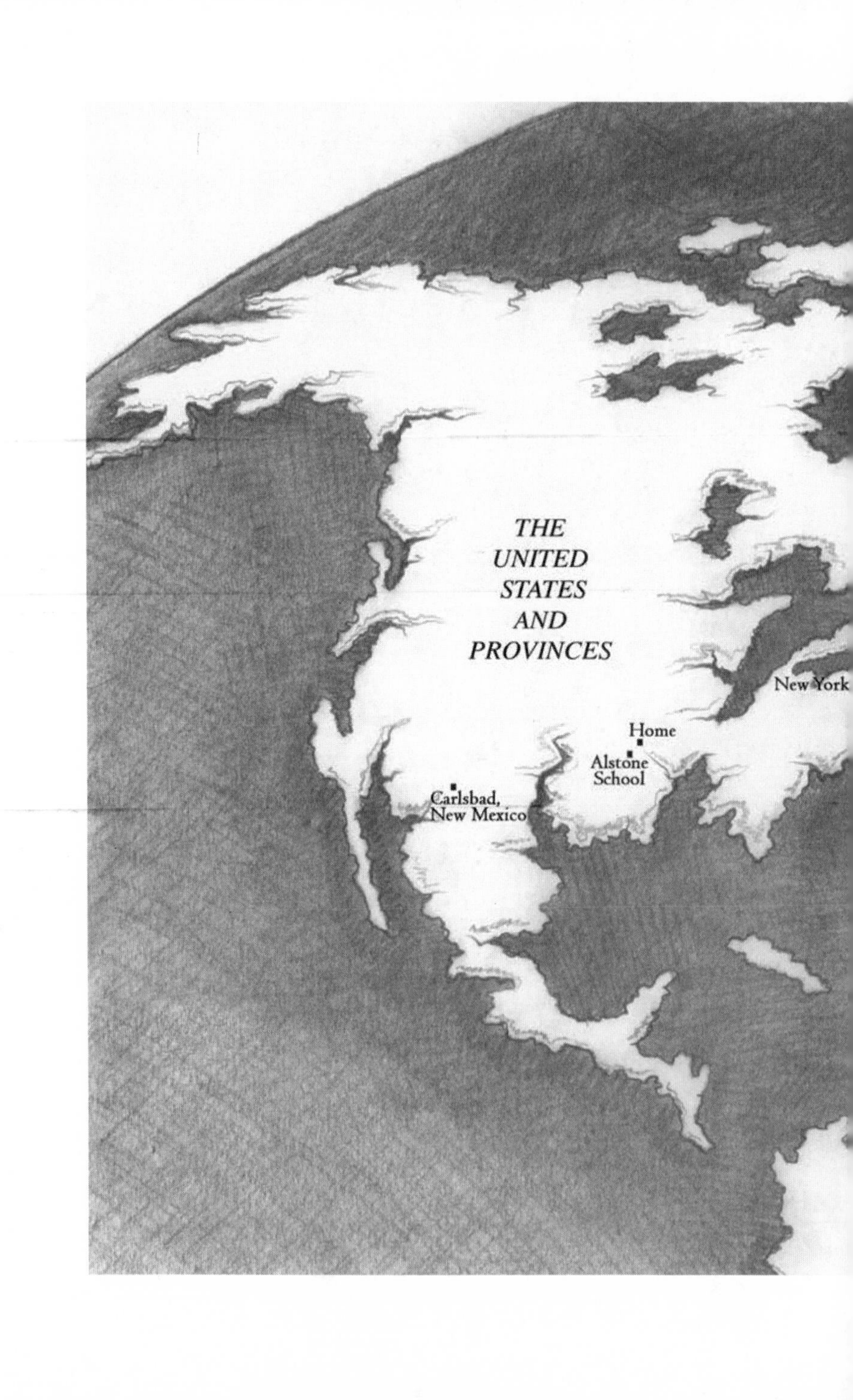
THE
UNITED
STATES
AND
PROVINCES
New York
Home
Alstone
School
Carlsbad,
New Mexico

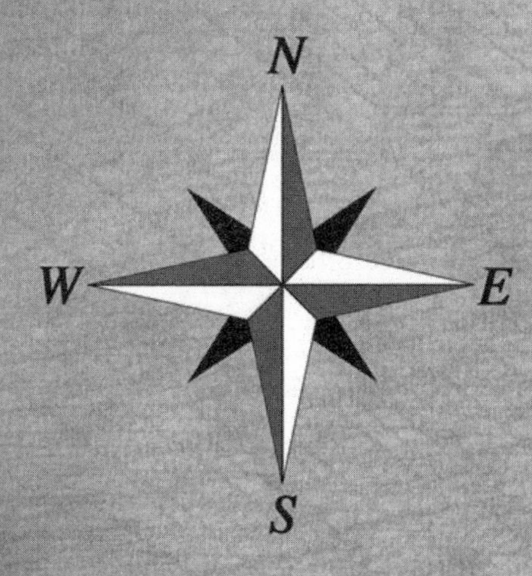
GREENLAND
UNGAVA
BAY
LIBRE
ATLANTIC OCEAN
N
W
E
S

CAST OF CHARACTERS

Dresdale Hamilton – One of your two best friends.

Peter Kim – Your other best friend.

Mr. Cummings – Headmaster of The Alstone School.

Dr. Heinrich Schliemann – Head of the Federal Historical Accuracy Board.

Dianna Torman – Your mother; she works with your father as an archaeologist. Most recently, they have been working on a special dig in and around Carlsbad Caverns, New Mexico.

Donald Torman – Your father; he works with your mother as an archaeogeologist.

Preston Billings – Financial adviser to your parents.
He works in NYC.

Lucas Foren – Head mechanic for a government vehicle depot, Brooklyn, New York.

Uncle Harry – Not your actual uncle; he is a friend of your parents in New Mexico.

Alphonse Rimy – A teacher at your school.

Captain DesLauriers – Captain of the *Northern Star*, an ice-skimming hovercraft in the Arctic.

Neila – One of the Illuminated.

Durno – Your Lemurian guide.

TABLE OF CONTENTS

FOREWORD TO THE SERIES

by R. A. Montgomery

NO TIME. NO SPACE.
ETERNITY HAD NOT BEGUN.

Perhaps there was a shuddering, a tremor, a forewarning of something enormous about to occur where no occurrence had ever been?

Without time we cannot now say that it was a billionth of a second when an event without precedent occurred. Was it a BANG? Was there noise where there was nothing?

Something happened. Something occurred. Some huge inevitability or responsibility or culpability started from no-start. Matter collected and expanded and shattered and was strewn throughout nothing creating everything.

Expansion. Expansion at tremendous speed beyond our current concept of the speed of light. A coming together. Heat. Light. Movement. Mass. And TIME.

How could this be? How could this not be?

Galaxies formed and were scattered though non-space that had become space like pails full of powdery, white sand.

What we called stars, planets, asteroids, meteors—all now heaven-bound leapt into being. Was it energy that unified all this? Was it the energy now locked in an atom or the sub, sub, sub particles?

Energy was probably the spider web network that filled non-space. And on that delicate but non-destructible web galaxies struggled to gain some dominance—already competition had begun—for the energy that fueled them. There was communication between these billions of galaxies, for how could there not be? They were made of the same stuff at the same time and unified in a sea of energy. So, from afar, as if picking through dunes for the smallest piece of sand, our mind's eye sees planet Earth. So minor, so unimportant as if size were important that it could be ignored. But it can't be ignored.

Earth is as expansive as anything else. Now it is locked in a deadly contest for control of energy. What energy? You ask. A good question. For this energy that is sought after and fought for is like love—it lacks definition, it cannot be captured or manufactured, it can't be ordered. It exists, and those that try to control it will find themselves beyond all reach.

So, begins THE GOLDEN PATH. On the spinning orb of the small, small planet called Earth a titanic struggle is about to explode that will determine how energy will be seen for a small bit of eternity.

Earth is not alone in this struggle; others believe that they too have a stake in all this hub-bub in this ever-expanding gigantic universe.

And so they do.

Is there evil? Of course, if that is what you call it. Is there good?

Of course.

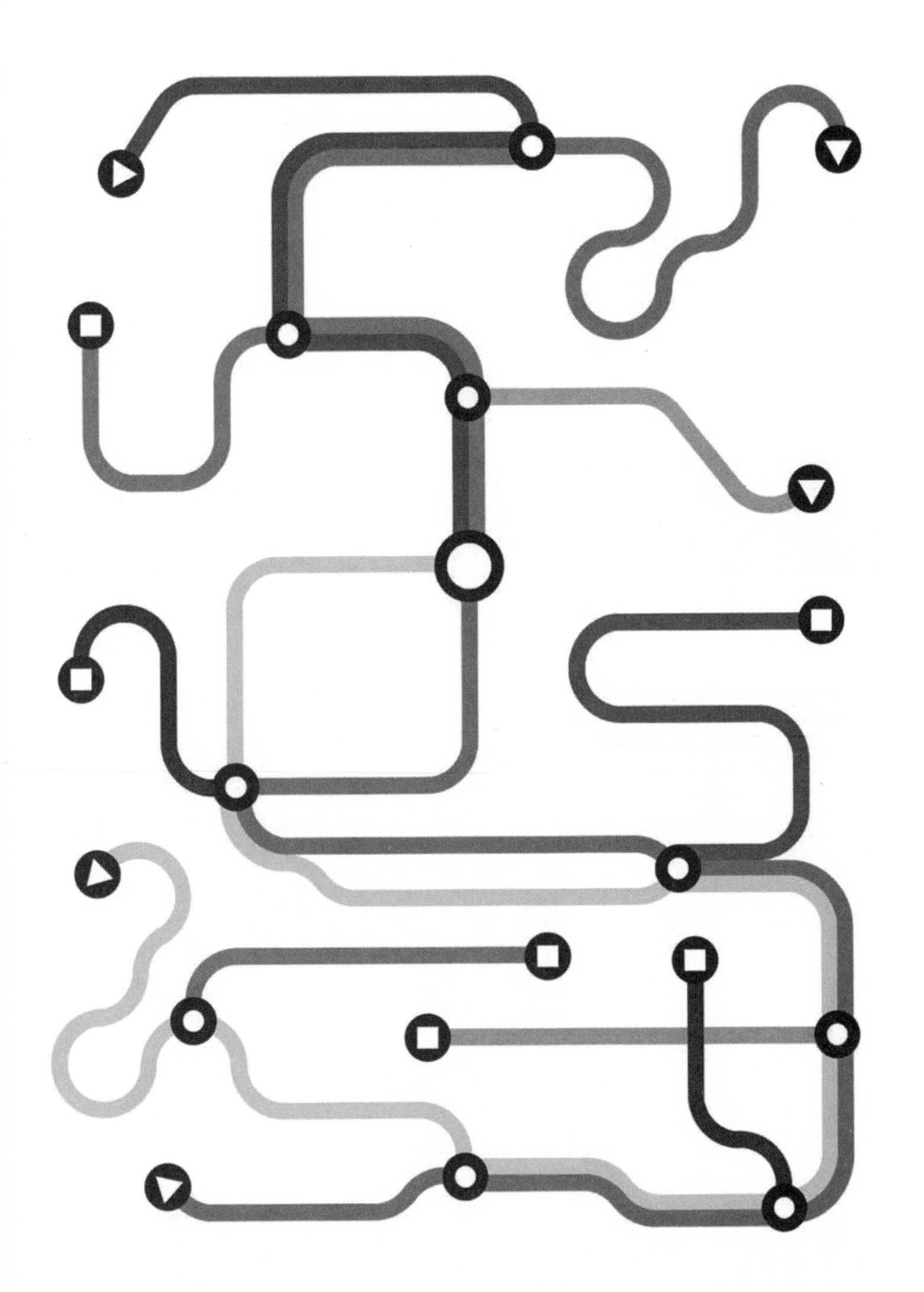

Change of Season

You and your friends Peter and Dresdale are sitting in the library of The Alstone School where you are boarding students. The three of you are studying for a trigonometry exam the next morning. The musty smell of the books is soothing and the warmth of the late afternoon sun makes you feel sleepy and content. You have a feeling you may ace your exam in the morning and that feeling is usually correct. Trying to focus on the task at hand, you listen to Dresdale teach Peter about the finer aspects of trig, but you find that your attention keeps wandering away from math problems. Your special history project will get its grade tomorrow, and you are really excited.

Over the past three months you and your two best friends have been working on analyzing an unusual pottery shard Peter found last summer. All three of you were interns at an archaeological and geological expedition to the Carlsbad Caverns in New Mexico run by your parents. Peter found the shard outside the caverns, on a hike through the backcountry. None of you had never seen anything like the writing you found on the odd-shaped shard of pottery. The three of you now think that it may come from a lost culture that came before the American Indians. You have titled your paper "The Forgotten People's Project."

Ms. Drenton, your AP history teacher, was very surprised when your group made your project proposal. Most students work solo, but she agreed to let the three of you work together. Dresdale was in charge of figuring out what the writing and images meant because she had the best knowledge of ancient languages and cultures. Peter was responsible for analyzing and dating the fragment. And you were in charge of writing the report and working on the main conclusions. Ms. Drenton said she might try and have it published if it was good enough.

"Sorry, Peter, but that one is wrong too," says Dresdale gently.

"Man! I just am so stupid! They are going to completely ask me not to come back after Christmas if I fail this dumb math course! Where will I go?" asks Peter with such pleading honesty that you snap out of your reverie and into the present.

"Peter, you are not stupid!" Dresdale says loudly. Other students turn their heads, but the head librarian, Mr. Tasker, is in the other room. Tasker is a really nice guy, but he freaks out on people who are loud. He fits the librarian stereotype so completely you wonder if he is just playing a part. "Trig is tricky," she continues in a lower voice. "You just need some extra time. Besides, you know you aren't dumb, you are the best computer geek in the whole school. Remember when the tech center had you paged during history class to go and rebuild their crashed server?"

"Yeah, but the trig exam is in the morning!" Peter whines.

Someone clears their throat. A Second Form girl with thick glasses appears behind Dresdale's chair.

"Aren't you the ones who spent the summer in Carlsbad?" she whispers.

You glance back and forth at Peter and Dresdale. The word about your special report has really gotten out.

"Yes, we are. Why?" Dresdale asks.

"I was on a government website just now and there's breaking news. A volcano exploded there today," she says, jerking her thumb over her shoulder toward an ancient Web terminal. Peter leaps up and hurries toward it before she can finish her sentence.

You and Dresdale are right behind.

"What kind of explosions? Where?" Dresdale demands as Peter rapidly types. She reads over his shoulder. "Volcanic? That doesn't make sense."

The three of you read the terse statement on an official government news site. Its short on details, as usual.

"Let's try The Gleamer," Peter says, typing in the address of an untraceable news site that usually has more accurate and detailed news. The Gleamer is run by "citizen journalists," people usually there at the scene of an event who don't trust the sanitized information the government deems okay. But all they have so far is a headline with "More to Come" underneath.

"What about your parents?" Dresdale asks, turning to you. "You should call to see if they are all right."

"I spoke to my parents two days ago," you reply. "They've been back home for the past two weeks," you explain. "But they probably know more than this. They would have called friends for information."

"Guys, check this out!" Peter interrupts. "Look at the official statement just issued by the Carlsbad Research Project Leader! Who is this Dr. Schliemann? Who is this guy? I thought your parents were in charge?"

You look down at the scratched screen of the Web terminal to where Peter is pointing.

Dr. H. Schliemann, Leader of the Carlsbad Expedition, issued this statement: "While we are grateful that no one was injured during this geological event, we want to make sure that the environment has stabilized. As a result, we are closing the cave complexes to the general public. We all hope that this closure will be as brief as possible."

"Who is this guy is right," you say aloud. Immediately you feel a hand on your shoulder. You see the stern, red face of Mr. Tasker looking down at you.

"*Out!*" he hisses quietly but emphatically.

All three of you scramble back to your table, gather up your stuff, and hustle out of the library. Mr. Tasker watches you intently until you step out of the door; his expression seems to say "you are not moving quickly or quietly enough!" You breathe in deeply as you step outside. Even though the sun is still strong, there is a nip to the fall air. It is nice, since cool days are fairly rare these days. You wonder if you will ever feel real cold with ice and driving snow.

"You can always count on them to not say anything about what really happened," complains Peter. "Something major must have happened for them to even acknowledge that something happened. But that Dr. Schliemann stuff was really strange. Have your parents said anything about this guy to you?"

"No," you answer. "They just said they were taking a break and going to work on some of the stuff they discovered back at the workshop at home. Not that they need any more junk cluttering up that place."

"Aren't you worried?" asks Dresdale.

Up until that moment, you hadn't been, but now you realize that maybe you should be worried. Your stomach gives a flip-flop. "Yeah, I am," you say. "They didn't say anything about being replaced. Everything sounded completely normal the other day."

"Parents are like that, sometimes," says Dresdale philosophically. "When my parents were breaking up, they kept pretending that everything was fine in front of us kids. We believed it for a long time, but at the end, we just wanted to shout. 'Quit pretending to like each other! We can hear you yelling at each other from the other room.' "

"I wouldn't know," mutters Peter, looking at his scruffy sneakers.

You wave to one of your teachers as the three of you slowly make your way to the dining hall. His name is Alphonse Rimy, but everyone just calls him Rimy. When you first saw Rimy at school three years ago, you thought he was part of the groundskeeping crew. He was wearing blue jeans and a denim jacket, and his hair was unkempt and greasy; not exactly the tweed jacket and pipe attire of the typical faculty member. But he has turned into one of your favorite teachers. Rumor says he could be teaching at any of the major universities but prefers to work with younger students. When you think about his challenging lectures and assignments, you can believe it.

"Hey, wait up!" shouts someone from behind you. You turn around and see an underclassman whose name you forget running toward the three of you. "Oh, great, you're all together!" He is panting and gasping as though he has been running for a while. "Sorry, just let me catch my breath. There. Anyway, all three of you have to report to the headmaster's office right away!"

"But dinner is about to start, and it's pizza night!" says Peter, continuing to walk toward the dining hall.

"He said to come right away," the underclassman replies. "There were a bunch of strange people standing there and he looked pretty serious. I would get there ASAP!"

"Maybe the Forgotten People's project won an award and they want to tell us in person?" you say with hope in your voice.

"Yeah, maybe," says Peter turning around and heading toward the headmaster's office with sloping shoulders and a dragging walk. "Or maybe they've decided to kick me out before I even get to take the stupid test, 'cause they know I'm going to fail it."

"Let's just move along and get this over with," says Dresdale nervously. You and Peter hurry to catch up with her as she strides toward the Schoolhouse and the headmaster's office. Taking the broad stone steps two at a time, Dresdale enters the building and heads straight to the office of Headmaster Cummings. You haven't spent too much time with the headmaster, but he has always seemed like a nice enough person, if a bit distracted. His secretary, Mrs. Hernandez, looks up at you as you enter his waiting room. She normally smiles, but she is not smiling now.

"What's up, Mrs. H?" says Peter.

"I'm not sure, Peter," she replies with a frown. "I'll tell Mr. Cummings you are here."

Mr. Cummings appears immediately and ushers the three of you into his office. It is neat and tidy, and he motions for you to take a seat. He is sweating. His normally kindly face is pinched and flushed and his white hair is in disarray. "Thank you for coming here so quickly, students," he says. "I suppose you have enjoyed your prank and were wondering when we would catch on?" He combs his fingers through his hair in an effort to bring it under control.

"What prank?" all three of you say together.

"Come now, enough is enough! Poor Ms. Drenton is very upset. You have tricked her quite cruelly!"

"What are you talking about?" you manage to say.

"Fine, continue to play your game then," the headmaster replies icily. "But we have proof that you stole the shard you are using for your Forgotten People's Project in Ms. Drenton's class."

"We didn't ste..." you begin, but Mr. Cummings interrupts you.

"I will give you one last chance to admit that you stole this artifact from the Carlsbad expedition and that you fabricated all of the research you submitted. If you do so, I can have this handled quietly. If not, I will convene the discipline board and it may go even further than that."

"No!" you say. "I don't know who is telling you this, but none of this is true."

"What do the two of you have to say?" says Mr. Cummings, looking at Dresdale and Peter. "I know that you two were not the main planners of this fraud, and if you confess now, the punishment will be much lighter for you. If not, the three of you will be expelled together."

"Sir, there must be some mistake, but none of this is true, we didn't do anything wrong!" You can hear the panic in Dresdale's voice. She is one of the hardest-working, and smartest, students that you know. Getting kicked out of school would be the worst thing in the world to her.

Peter tries to speak, but nothing but a wet gurgling comes out of his mouth. You can tell that he is mad. "Wh…wh. . whhaat, what are you saying!?" he finally manages to yell. "We haven't done anything. How dare you scare Dresdale and us like that! She is the best student this stupid school has!"

Cummings takes a deep breath, as if he's trying to control his temper. "Fine. I tried to help you out," he says. His voice and manner are even colder than before. "But since you won't accept it, I have no choice but to bring you before the Discipline Board."

As if in a dream, the three of you are then led to a small room off from the teachers' conference room. None of you know what to say to each other. Peter slams his fist into his palm while Dresdale keeps repeating "This can't be happening" to herself in a small voice.

Within minutes, you find yourself watching a tall man dressed in an expensive suit tell the discipline board that you and your friends had stolen a rare prehistoric artifact from the expedition site.

"I am Dr. Heinrich Schliemann," he announces in finishing. "I work with the Federal Historical Accuracy Board."

Heinrich Schliemann? Dr. H. Schliemann? The guy you just read about online, the one who released the "official" statement about the volcanic explosion? You glance around and notice three large, tough-looking men in suits hanging in the back of the room. You hadn't seen them when you came in. They don't talk or smile. You think they look like bodyguards.

"That's the guy who took your parents' job!" whispers Peter, nudging you in the ribs and pointing. "What's he doing here?"

"He's creepy," Dresdale agrees in a low whisper. "Look at the way he's sliming up to Ms. Drenton!"

Dr. Schliemann, leaning toward Ms. Drenton, raises his voice for a moment. "That is why, I must insist that these students be expelled and given into the custody of the Federal Historical Accuracy Board to face trial for their crimes!"

"But they're just children," protests Ms. Drenton weakly. "Even if they knew what they were doing, they don't deserve to go to jail!"

"Are you aware of the value of this shard of pottery?" asks Schliemann, holding up the hand-sized, irregular shaped triangle of pottery that you have gotten to know so well.

"I am a history teacher," she replies dryly. "I hope I under-

stand the importance of historical objects."

"I don't think you really understand the true value of this particular shard. This piece is the keystone to the rest of a vessel. A very important ancient vessel. That is why we need to take them into our custody, so we can find out if there are any other pieces that they may have taken...finding all of the pieces is extremely urgent!" he says menacingly.

"Come now, Dr. Schliemann. we here at Alstone realize the seriousness of this charge. And, we are aware of the power you and your friends wield. But you can't just waltz in to my school and grab three students!" interjects Mr. Cummings.

"Besides, you haven't even listened to our side of the story!" says Dresdale standing up. You recognize that fierce Dresdale look and she's got it now. "This Dr. Schliemann person is lying to you. We haven't stolen anything!"

"Dresdale is right," chimes in Peter. "I found the shard far away from the expedition site this summer! I would guess more than a mile from the perimeter. I was taking a hike through the desert scrub and I found it just lying there. I didn't steal it from anywhere!"

You are so shocked that you can't even speak. Why are you having to defend yourself against these bizarre charges? You look at the teachers on the discipline board. Even Coach Richardson, who has always liked you and helped you even though you aren't a star soccer player, is glaring at you as if you have let him down. He shakes his head at you when you catch his eye.

"Peter! Dresdale! Be quiet!" shouts Mr. Cummings. "You will have your chance. I don't think you know quite how serious this is. Lying will only make it worse. Dr. Schliemann has provided clear proof that the shard was stolen from the excavation site, and that the theft was done knowingly and surreptitiously."

Schliemann gives you a cold smile, and you see his dark eyes laughing at you. "If you found the shard, then, why didn't you report it to the expedition leaders?" He asks the question quietly, but you can hear the threat behind it.

"We wanted to work on examining the shard by ourselves," you hear yourself explaining. "It was going to be a surprise when we submitted our paper for publication." You decide to leave the part about surprising your parents out of it.

"Very convenient," says Schliemann. "Surely you must have

had some sort of guess as to the fragment's value? Ancient writing and pictographs like nothing else? Of course, you also know about the Antiquities and Historical Objects law? All antiquities of value are the property of the United States and Provinces government, no matter where they are discovered."

"We were going to hand it over!" protests Peter. "We didn't know how valuable it was at first. It was only after we started studying it that we realized how… strange it is."

"As I said before: very convenient," Heinrich Schliemann says. "Criminals are always on their way to return the stolen goods when they are caught."

"We are *not* criminals," Dresdale says, glaring at Schliemann. He takes a step back and then steps forward purposefully as if to show that he is not afraid of her.

"You'll think differently once you are locked in a cell!" Schliemann snarls. Then he smiles and laughs.

"Sit down, Dresdale!" scolds Mr. Cummings. "Dr. Schliemann, don't push too far. These are minor children, and we still have some rights left to us. I think I have the consensus of the board that we need to expel all three students immediately." He looks around and you see Ms. Drenton, Coach Richardson, and the others nod. You can't believe that no one is defending you. Your heart feels sick. While you have hated being at boarding school many times, the thought of leaving, being kicked out, scares you.

"However," continues Mr. Cummings. "I can't in good faith place these minor children into your custody unless you can convince the police or Gatekeepers to come and get them. The Federal Historical Accuracy Board doesn't have those powers. At least not yet."

"Fine. But this isn't over," Schliemann answers. He turns in your direction. "I'll come find you and the next time you won't have any way to get away," Schliemann says, picking up his black leather briefcase and stalking to the door. In his haste, he leaves a pile of papers on the table. His goons follow, but not before all three of them take long looks at you and your friends. You get the feeling they are trying to memorize what you look like. It gives you shivers.

The members of the Discipline Board file out of the room in silence. No one looks at you. You feel like crying but you manage to hold it back.

"Please come with me," says Mr. Cummings to the three of you. "I've arranged to have a faculty member take you to your house. You need to leave tonight." Then, under his breath, and sounding like an apology, he adds, "It's the best I can do for you."

"You don't really believe what they said about us, do you?" you say, staring Mr. Cummings straight in the face. He flushes and turns away.

"You need to leave the school tonight," is his only reply.

Less than two hours after being told to go to the headmaster's office, you, Peter and Dresdale find yourselves packed and getting ready to leave the school that has been your home for the last three years. Since Peter doesn't really have a home and he usually stays vacations with you, and because Dresdale's home is half a continent away, you have decided to all go to your house, which is only three hours away by surface car. You tried calling your parents to tell them the bad news, but no one answered. You know that they won't mind having Peter and

Dresdale stay with you for a few days. There is plenty of room, and you're sure that your parents will want to talk to all three of you about the accusations.

"Just take what you really need," says a gravelly voice from the hallway.

"Who's there?" you ask.

"It's me," says Alphonse Rimy as he walks into the chaos of your room. "I'm here to take you to your parents' house. We can't seem to get through to them, and we can't send three minors off by themselves without supervision. I'm willing to make the drive to see if we can find your parents. It's not like them to..." he mutters and sort of rambles off.

Normally you might have wondered what Rimy was talking about, but you have just been kicked out of school, Your head is still spinning with the utter unbelievability of it all.

"Ok," you say, glad at least that the ride will be with a teacher who's sympathetic.

"I have the necessary papers and clearances for the journey if we run into the Gatekeepers or other units from Travel Control," Rimy adds.

You look Rimy in the eye when you remember. "First I need to get one last thing," you say.

"Come on!" Peter urges as you look down the hall in front of the teacher's conference room. No one is around. "Hurry up!"

You open the door, and your eyes immediately go to the table where Schliemann sat. There it is! He left the shard on the table after the discipline board had dismissed the meeting. It is covered by a stack of papers, but you know exactly where to look. You can't believe that Schliemann would leave the shard, but there it is. It feels warm and smooth in your hand.

Moving quickly, you put the shard in your pocket, grab Peter gently by the arm, and walk out. "Where's Rimy?" you ask Dresdale when you join her in the parking lot behind the dining hall. "I thought he said to meet him here."

"It was strange. I was waiting here for you guys, when Rimy drove up and told me that he couldn't go with us after all. He shoved these travel clearance papers into my hand and told me that he was going to Ungava Bay to help his sick mother. He said that it was essential that we get out of here and go to your parents. He said to just take Peter's car. Then he took off. He looked stressed and in a hurry." Dresdale shoves her hands into the front pocket of her hooded sweatshirt and looks at Peter expectantly.

"I'm not sure my heap of rust will make it, but we may as well get going before someone comes and tells us to go with someone else. Rimy is about the only teacher I trust right now," says Peter, pausing for a moment. "But it's really strange that he said he had to go see his sick mother."

"Why?" you ask.

"We've talked a lot about different things through the years," Peter answers. "He once told me he was an orphan too."

"That's really weird," you say.

"Just like this whole day," Dresdale adds.

"I don't know which way is up, but if the school doesn't

want me, then I don't want to stay here another second," you announce. "Let's go get Peter's car. How did Rimy know that you had a car anyway? I thought Dresdale and I were the only ones who knew."

"Like I said, we talked about a lot of things." Peter answers.

The three of you leave the school grounds and start the two-mile walk into town. You turn and look back at the sun setting against the Schoolhouse bell tower, and you wonder if you will ever see Alstone again. Somehow, you are not sure if you want to or not.

"Hey Peter," says Dresdale brightly. "I have some good news."

"Please don't hold it back, I could use every bit that you have."

"None of us have to take that trig test tomorrow," says Dresdale.

"Thanks, Dres, I hadn't thought of that."

You think back to the feeling you had back in the warmth of the library just a few hours ago. How can things change so quickly? Your feeling that you were going to ace a test had never let you down before. You didn't even get a chance to take it and now you probably never will. Something very like the opposite feeling from earlier enters into you like a cold or sickness. You get a terrible feeling that things are not going to be getting better for a long time.

The three of you walk quickly and you soon warm up in the cool night air. Moving your body feels good, and you are almost disappointed when you get to the rear employee's parking lot of the Strafford Inn, where Peter has his car stashed. The last of the sun has faded and the first stars are showing in the clear sky.

"Do you have enough fuel?" you ask as he warms up the engine of the old car. It started out life as a regular gasoline car, but it had been converted to Synth-Fuel use over twenty years ago. Peter's grandfather had owned the car, and when he passed away two years ago, Peter got it since his parents were both dead. It was the only thing he had that was truly and completely his own. Even though its rusty panels and mismatched paint jobs made it look laughable, Peter loved his car with a deep passion.

"She's got half a tank. Should be more than enough to get there," says Peter with pride. "She gets good mileage."

Dresdale smiles at him.

Peter knows the way to your house, and he drives swiftly but safely on the monitored lanes. You do have the travel papers that Rimy gave Dresdale, but you don't want the Gatekeeper goons to start asking why three kids are traveling alone after dark. Everyone wanted to avoid the Gatekeepers. They were like the police, but scarier. Their job seemed to be less and less about protecting people, and more and more about controlling people. Travel and communications in particular had been restricted. It was all done in the name of "security."

Peter cranks up the heat as the night gets colder, but the old car struggles to put out much heat. The cold only came that morning; before then it had been scorching hot. You notice the landmarks of the drive that you have taken from school to home over the last three years. Your stomach clenches as you wonder if you will ever drive back this way again.

"I can't believe the Discipline Board bought that load of crap the Schliemann guy was selling," Peter says with deep bitterness. "Who the hell is he anyway?"

"The whole thing was surreal," agrees Dresdale. "It seemed to me that Cummings and the other teachers were afraid of Schliemann. None of the normal protocols were followed. We haven't even been able to tell your parents that we are coming, but they let the three of us just walk off of campus into the night. It's all very strange."

"Cummings seemed nervous alright, but I couldn't tell by what. He seemed relieved to see us go, not mad about that stupid stealing charge," you say.

"What is the Federal Historical Accuracy Board anyway? I've never heard of it, and I know most of the strange little agencies that pull the strings from the edges," asks Dresdale rhetorically, knowing that if she does not know it, you two definitely do not. "How can they just come into school and get us kicked out in a matter of hours?"

"Maybe it has something to do with the insurgency? The FFA have been pretty active lately," you say. "Nothing on the official broadcasts, but rumors have been spreading about major attacks on both sides."

All three of you fall silent at that thought. If you were part of the insurgency, all bets were off. The government could, and did, use "extraordinary measures" to fight what it called "traitors and seditious elements." The Freedom Forever Alliance, or the FFA, for short, had originally been a guerrilla movement. Recently they seemed much better equipped and trained. You heard your dad call the Gatekeepers' response to the FFA a "modern day inquisition." Sometimes people just went missing. At school this fall you heard other students talking about Gatekeepers showing up in the dead of night to take people away. When rumors like that reached the student body of Alstone, things had to be getting bad out in the real world.

Just as you are remembering these gloomy thoughts, you see the familiar turn off to your street and breathe a sigh of relief. No matter what is going on in your life, you always feel better once you get home. You're scared to tell your parents that you've been expelled, but you're eager to see them and ask for their advice and support. And find out more about Schliemann!

The lights in the house and in the garage workshop are all off, which is strange, as it's only 10:30 PM. Your mom is always up later than that. Peter pulls up to the house and you open the door and jump out. The front door is locked. You get the key from the fake rock and open the door.

"Mom? Dad? It's me, I'm home from school," you yell out into the dark house. You flip the lights on. "Peter and Dresdale are with me! I hope that's okay."

You are greeted by total silence.

"Mom? Dad?" you holler again.

"Maybe they've gone out?" says Peter walking into the kitchen. Everything is clean, but the flowers in the vase are dry and brown. Dead flowers are not allowed in your mom's kitchen. She doesn't seem to mind the massive clutter in her workshop, but your mother always makes sure that the kitchen is ready for an impromptu cooking show to descend and demand to be let into her kitchen.

"Hey," says Dresdale, tugging at your sleeve and looking out the window above the kitchen sink looking to your parents' workshop and the garage. "I think I just saw someone walking by the garage."

"Maybe they're out there," you say. "But why would they keep the lights off? I'm going to go check it out."

Peter grabs your mom's mean-looking cleaver and says, "I'm coming with you."

"Me too," Dresdale says.

"Okay," you say as you head into the cool night. "Don't stab someone by accident, Peter."

"If I stab someone it will be purely on purpose," he says cockily before adding. "Don't worry, I won't do anything stupid. I just have an odd feeling."

"You can't stab someone with a cleaver," Dresdale says. "It's meant for chopping."

"Shhh."

You look in the windows of the two-bay garage but you don't see anything strange. Both of your parents' cars are gone. Piles of junk form strange shapes that don't allow you to see what's what, so you open the door of the garage using the keyless touchpad to turn on the light. As soon as the door rumbles open and the light turns on someone inside the garage starts screaming. You see someone scramble to their feet and rush toward you.

"Stop barking! Stop barking stop barking stop *barking!*" yells

your neighbor Tommy into your face.

"Hold on Peter!" you shout. "It's just my neighbor, Tommy. He's not going to hurt us."

"What's going on, Tommy?" You say the words gently and carefully. Tommy is twelve years old, and autistic. He can't communicate well at the best of times and almost never if he's upset. Brown hair falls into his pale green eyes. He looks and sounds normal enough until he begins to repeat himself obsessively.

"What happened? Who is barking?" you ask Tommy again. That's when you remember that your mom's dog, Tito, wasn't inside the house either. "Is Tito barking?"

"Stop barking!" Tommy shouts. He looks away from you and flaps his hands in frustration. He is definitely upset. "What happened?" you ask again. "Who stopped barking? Was it Tito?"

While you and Peter are talking to Tommy, Dresdale has gone ahead and opened up the door to your parents' workshop and turned on the lights.

"Oh no!" she gasps. "Come quickly!"

"Stop *barking!*" yells Tommy.

"It's okay, Tommy," says Peter.

On the floor of your parents' workshop, you see the small lifeless form of Tito. His brown body is curled up and his pink tongue is hanging out of his mouth. He doesn't move. You run forward and kneel down by his side. Tito isn't breathing and his tongue is swollen and dry. "Tito," you moan softly, "poor little guy."

"Is he dead?" Peter asks, resting his hand on your shoulder and peering down at the small body.

"Yes, he's gone," you say softly, feeling both sad and scared. You never completely bonded with Tito. He was small and yapped a lot. Your mother got him the second year you were away at boarding school. You missed Tito's puppyhood, but he could be sweet sometimes. He always loved it when you scratched his belly. No matter what, nothing deserved to die like he had.

"It looks like dehydration," Dresdale says. "He must have been locked up in here."

"Come back later. Stop barking! Stop barking!" Tommy says as he comes into the workshop. "Yeeeaargggh!" he says when he sees Tito's body. "Tito!"

"Hey Tommy," you say gently, fighting back tears that surprise you. "What happened here? Where are my parents?"

"Come back! Stop barking!" says Tommy, looking away from you and giving a little jump. "Leaves fall in the night. Leaves fall in the night. Come back, stop barking. Stop barking. Tito."

"It's okay, Tommy, why don't you go home? It's late and I'm sure your parents are worried about you."

You look up at Peter and Dresdale. This is serious. "I think something happened to my mom and dad. No way would my mom leave Tito without food or water, or even with food or water. She takes him everywhere. Dad calls Tito the 'Baby Replacement Project.'" You try to laugh, but it comes out as a choking sound.

"I think something has happened to them, too," Dresdale says.

"Let's search the house," Peter says. He moves the cleaver from hand-to-hand nervously. Tommy shies away from the knife.

You look at your two best friends. "Let's check the workshop first and then we will search the house. First I'll take Tommy home."

You guide the autistic boy down the path that leads to his house through a small patch of woods and return to the workshop. Dresdale and Peter have taken three steps inside and stopped.

"It's much cleaner than it usually is," Dresdale comments, looking around.

You nod and scan the room.

"We probably shouldn't touch anything," Peter suggests.

He's right. This could be a crime scene. You carefully tread the perimeter of the space. It's filled with the usual artifacts and samples in various stages of study and cataloging. Some pottery shards are getting a bath in a gentle acid wash.

"Look," Peter says, pointing. "That's odd."

There is a smudged footprint of a workboot in the corner, but it's hard to tell how old it is. When you have traversed the entire space, you notice that Dresdale has taken a towel from the bathroom and wrapped Tito's body up into a small bundle.

Staying together, the three of you move back to the house.

"Let's start in the kitchen," you say. You carefully go through the room, opening cupboards and the refrigerator. Everything is clean and organized. The milk is dated to go bad this Friday. You continue on into the library, dining room, and den. However, nothing is really out of place. A few things are in the wrong places, but nothing that could not have happened in the months that you have been away at school. You move to the hallway and go straight to the old gothic-style mirror.

"My mom always told me to look here for any special

messages she or my dad might have for me," you explain as you reach behind the mirror, searching for the pouch on its back. "I thought it was just for fun, but maybe she left something there?"

There is nothing in the pouch behind the mirror though.

You head up the stairs and go through your parents' bedroom next. Their room seems spooky, probably because of Tito's death, or murder. The absence of your parents hangs like a fog over everything.

"Toothbrushes are here," Dresdale announces from the master bath. "And the rest of their toiletries. They didn't expect to be away long."

"Something is very wrong about all of this," Peter intones softly. All thoughts about being kicked out of Alstone are gone. That's kids' stuff in comparison; this has the cold and moist feeling of evil reality.

You quickly scan the rest of the upstairs rooms. Nothing.

"Log onto the Net and see if they sent you an email?" Peter says when you are downstairs back in the kitchen.

"Good thinking. I should have done it earlier!" You pull out your laptop from your backpack and log on. Its case is scratched and dented from two years of abuse, but it still works fine.

The first email you get is from the school, officially notifying you and your parents about your expulsion. As painful as that still is, considering that it only happened earlier that day, you rush to the email from your mother as soon as you see her name. At first glance you thought it might be spam, as it is not her work email address:

FROM: Dianna Torman dtorman@deadmail.anonymous.guyana.000
SUBJECT: Something has happened to us.

Sweetheart, I don't want to alarm you, but I fear I must. If you are getting this email it is because something has happened to us. It is rigged to be sent from a special "dead drop" anonymous server if I have not checked back in three days. Your father and I have been afraid that people were moving against us after we were removed from heading the Carlsbad dig. I can't get too specific because I do not know myself who exactly is targeting us. We will try and contact you as soon as we are able.

Leave school and go see your Uncle Harry in Carlsbad. He works in the branch office of the Federal Historical Accuracy Board and he can help you. His work address is: FHAB District Office, Harold Turner, 224 Mesa Street, Suite B11, Carlsbad, NM.

Don't call him or email him, just go see him as soon as possible!

Use the flyer at home if you can. It has enough fuel to get to Carlsbad, and its transponder codes have been authorized to fly there. Don't try going anywhere else though, as the Gatekeepers will immediately stop you. They keep a tight leash on all flyers.

Rimy can give you a ride home from school; he is a trusted friend. Just tell him I asked him as a "special boon."

I will try and leave a more detailed note in the secret spot. There is much your father and I need to explain to you, but I can't really explain until I see you in person. I can't wait until I see your beautiful face! Be strong, be brave, and know that your father and I love you more than life itself! I am sorry to scare you with this news, but it will all work out in the end!!!!

Love,
Mom

"I think I'm going to be sick," you moan as soon as you finish your mom's email. Maybe this is just some big joke? But Tito's death is no joke, and nothing about this day has been very funny. "I don't even have an Uncle Harry."

The phone rings and all three of you jump. You look at the caller ID, and it says: Billings, Palmer and Polk.

"It's my parents' financial advisor. He calls all the time, but why would he be calling at midnight?"

"Hello?" you say into the mouthpiece.

"It's Preston Billings here, are your parents home? I need to talk to Dianna or Donald immediately."

"No, Mr. Billings, they're not here. I don't know where they are. I think they are in trouble." Billings has always been nice to you, but you don't know why you tell him that.

"What do you mean in trouble?" he asks. "They were on their way to meet me here tonight. In New York City. But they never showed up. God! I hate that they outlawed cell phones. All for safety!" He gives a bitter laugh.

"Why were they coming to meet you?" you ask.

"I think it would be best if you came here to New York City. I have some new information for your parents that is very important to all of you."

"I think someone has taken them," you say weakly, voicing your fear for the first time. "We found my mom's dog Tito dead in their workshop. The house is. . .neat but everything just seems strange."

There's a long pause.

"Honestly, I think you need to get out of there right now,"

Mr. Billings says urgently. "I can arrange a travel document via email. Do you have a car?"

"Yes," you answer. Peter and Dresdale are staring at you with intense eagerness, but they are keeping silent and following your lead. You haven't mentioned them yet. "Mr. Billings, I am not sure I should tell you this, but my mom sent an email that would only be triggered if they were in trouble. I just read it. She says I need to go meet with someone in Calsbad, some friend of theirs."

"Don't go to Carlsbad!" he says. "Not with the explosion. It's is too dangerous now! Listen, give me your email address and I'll send the travel documents in the morning. Right now I want you to get out of there."

"Why?" you ask. You have a flashback to that afternoon when you first saw the tall figure of Dr. Schliemann.

"I really can't talk over the phone," Billings replies. "Please take my word for it. I'll email you the documents. Get out of there as quickly as possible."

The phone line goes dead.

You are stunned. Things seem to be moving fast, and in the wrong direction. You look at your two friends.

"What do we do? This flyer your mom mentioned in her email, how did they get it?" Peter asks.

"The government gave them a low-level flyer for the excavation they did in Belize. They didn't use it much at the Carlsbad dig. It should fit the three of us with room for half a toothbrush."

"What did that Billings guy say?" Dresdale asks.

"He said we should get out of here as soon as possible and go to New York City to meet him. He says he has information for my parents. They were scheduled to be there to meet him tonight. He also said 'don't go to Carlsbad.'" Your head pulses with a weary ache, but your heart and stomach feel much worse

"I hate to say this, but I am going to faint if I don't get some food," says Peter. Dresdale glares at him. "What?" he asks defensively. "I haven't eaten since we had mac and cheese at the dining hall for lunch."

"No, you're right. We need to get some food and get out of here," you say. "But where do we go?"

"Can you operate the flyer?" Dresdale asks.

"It's mostly automated, but my dad let me take it into manual mode a couple of times. You don't get very high off the ground and if the power quits it has a backup elevation field that brings you down easy. Where do you guys think I should go?"

"What do you mean, 'I'?" says Dresdale. "We're coming with you."

"Yeah," agrees Peter. "But after we get some food!"

"These are my problems. You two should go to Dresdale's mom's house," you reply. "I've gotten you in enough trouble. I'll take care of this."

"Don't be nuts. We're not going to let you go off by yourself. Anyway, I'm not sure what is going on, but somehow I think that we are all in this together," Dresdale says, and her face looks so earnest and caring that you feel almost good for a second. Then reality comes crashing down again.

"So where are we going? Do we listen to the email from my mom and take the flyer or listen to Billings and go to the Big Soggy Apple?"

If you choose to follow your mother's plea in the dead-drop email and go to Carlsbad to meet Uncle Harry, turn to page 52.

If your gut tells you to go to New York City to meet Preston Billings and learn his "important information," turn to page 43.

Child of the Child

The metal links of the chain fence are cool to your touch, even though the day is already warm. You scramble up the fence, using your best monkey skills as your heart beats rapidly. Peter and Dresdale both get over the top before you, and you slide over mere seconds after them. You scrape your leg as you swing it over the top, but you don't have time to worry. Three men are positioned in front of you.

"Run!" you yell.

You run toward what looks like an abandoned factory. The windows are smashed and the front door is ajar. Dresdale reaches the door first and opens it. A broken padlock hangs forlornly from the hasp. You hear a sound.

"Oh, no! They just rammed the car through the fence! We need to get out of here!"

"Did they see us come in here?" Peter asks.

"I don't know," you answer, scanning the dusty room. "But I think that we have to get out of here ASAP!"

"Yeah, let's move it."

"We came in the front door. There must be a back door. Come on!"

There is an emergency exit in the back stairwell. You yank at it, but it doesn't budge.

"This door's locked!" you complain to Peter, as if it was his fault.

"We'll go out this window," Dresdale announces calmly as she uses a broom handle to clear out broken glass from a small window looking out onto an alley.

You get a bad cut getting through the window, and this one feels wet and throbs nastily. But you don't have time to worry about it. Peter waves at you frantically from further down the alley. You rush to meet him before the goons find your blood trail.

"In here," Dresdale whispers as you round the corner.

Next to a large building is a small shed filled with rusty pipes and gratings. The three of you squirm under a dusty blue tarp and try and get as comfortable as you can while lying on sharp bits of metal. It's hot in the shed, and blood drips from your elbow.

"Are you sure we should hide here?"

"Shh!"

"I don't know," Peter whispers back, "but shut up, would you? We're here now."

You feel like screaming, but you don't. People search outside the shed. They open the shed door; you can tell because the reflected light off the dirty floor is enough to let you see. The three of you hold your breath. Finally they move on. By the time you leave the shed, the sun is falling in the sky and the temperature is dropping.

"Do you think they're out there?" Peter squeaks.

"Don't know," Dresdale says as she chews on her hair. "But we should get out of here. What time are we supposed to meet Uncle Harry?"

"Five-thirty. But I need some food first," you answer, walking quickly away from the factory buildings.

You don't have much money with you, and you know you should conserve it, but when you see the dusty taxi coming around the corner, you don't hesitate a moment before waving it down.

"Man, that is good!" Peter says, draining a plastic glass of iced tea in one long gulp. "Can I have a refill?" He asks the waitress with a smile. Somehow he again looks fresh and clean after a couple of minutes at the bathroom sink. You, however, look like the "before" part of a soap ad. The waitress smiles gently and takes his glass without saying anything and fills it up for him.

"I really, really, love Mexican food," you say, feeling much better after a large pork burrito with salsa, guacamole, onions, cheese and black beans. "How was your veggie one?" you ask Dresdale politely.

"Good. You always talk about food. We need to get to the storage unit. I don't think we should risk walking again."

"Already taken care of. I called a taxi when I went to the bathroom. I don't have much cash left, but there is no way that I am going to risk meeting up with those guys in the black car. It was strange. It was like we were playing hide and seek with them, and we were little kids. But I was scared. I know they would do something horrible to us, like torture us, or throw us off a cliff or something."

"Me too," Peter says. "I don't think those guys are kidding around."

"But don't always assume the worst. Maybe they just wanted to talk to us and then they would have let us go."

"Sure, Dres," Peter says, rolling his eyes and walking away from her. "Why don't you go find them and ask them about their plans?"

"I said I was glad that they didn't find us. Maybe you two are right, and I was scared too, but that doesn't mean that the worst would have happened."

"I see the cab," you interject.

You tell the cab driver the address and settle in on the taped-up backseat. Dresdale and Peter aren't talking to each other, so you sit uncomfortably in the middle and try and make small talk. You are kind of sick of their little tiffs. One or the other was always taking what the other said and making too big a deal about it. Dresdale thought Peter didn't listen to her shades of gray, while Peter would get forced into an unyielding corner of straightjacket logic.

"Fine," you say after more one-syllable answers from Dres and Peter. "Both of you be little babies and sulk. Meanwhile

I'm going to try and figure out who took my parents and killed Tito."

Your bitterness surprises you, but neither Dresdale nor Peter say anything in response. The cab pulls up to the U-Stor-It storage facility and you get out. The sun has disappeared behind some thick clouds in the western sky but it is still bright at the moment. Long shadows are faint but distinct, with sharp edges. You look around the storage facility. Except for the desert stretching out beyond the fenced-in area, you could be anywhere in the country.

"Dad used to have a storage unit before they built their workshop," you tell the still-silent Dresdale and Peter as you look for unit 34. "It was always filled with so much crap. Something about the whole thing always creeped me out. I was always thinking, maybe there are dead bodies hidden away in there in big plastic tubs."

"Great, thanks for making me feel creeped out, too." Dresdale says crossly. "Here it is."

You knock on the rolling metal doorway to the storage unit. "Uncle Harry? Are you there?"

The door lifts up suddenly from the inside.

"Quick!" Uncle Harry says as he pokes his head below the edge of the door. He grabs your hand and pulls you into the darkness of the storage unit. "Did anyone see you come? Who are your friends?"

He turns on an electric lamp and puts it on a shelf. Two other adults besides Uncle Harry are inside the storage unit with you.

"Who are your friends?" you ask defensively. The events of the day have made you wary.

"Fair enough," Harry replies. "This is François," he points to a tall bearded man who smiles but still looks scary. He extends his hand and you shake it. The hand is rough and calloused.

"Pleased to meet you," François says with a faint accent. You suspect that he is French or Quebecois, but mainly because of his first name.

"I'm Margaret Carlson. I'm president of the Carlsbad Institute. We are a think tank here in town. Call me Maggie. I knew your parents very well."

Even in the low light, you can see that Margaret Carlson is dressed professionally and neatly in an expensive tailored pantsuit. You are amazed that she is not sweating. Wait a second!

"What do you mean, you *knew* my parents? Are they okay?" Your heart beats with fear and guilt.

"Oh, don't worry! No. I'm sorry. I didn't mean to upset you. But… you know that your parents are missing, Harry told us that much," she looks at Peter and Dresdale and then she looks at you. "Are they okay to hear this?"

"Yes, yes, of course," you respond. "We were all kicked out of Alstone School together. Two days ago. Because of something connected to our internship here in Carlsbad last summer. Then we discovered my parents missing together…Please! Tell me what you know."

"Do you remember the section of the dig at Carlsbad

Cavern that was roped off for stability issues?" Harry says quickly.

"The Left-Hand Tunnel," Peter answers. "Roped off for safety but strangely filled with people."

"Right. Well," says Harry, warming to his role of storyteller. "It was a disguised special lab run by the FFA."

"You're part of the insurgency?!" blurts Dresdale. "Right under the noses of FHAB?" The three exchange glances. Maggie Carlson nods.

"You'd be surprised who has joined us, especially in the last couple of years," Maggie answers. "As things have gotten worse, people have lost their most basic rights."

"What does this have to do with my parents?" you ask.

"People like your parents," Harry says intently, "had had enough. We couldn't have kept the lab a secret without your parents' knowledge."

"And their help," Maggie says quietly, kneading her hands.

"Lab?" Dresdale asks. "The Left-Hand Tunnel contained a lab? Used for what?"

Harry and Maggie exchange looks. Harry takes a deep breath.

"They just called it a lab. It really contained a system of tunnels. We believe it was a transit system, an ancient one, using a sort of temperature-regulated vacuum system for power," Harry begins.

"Transit to where?" you ask.

"The Inner Earth," Maggie Carlson says.

You look back and forth at Peter and Dresdale.

"There's really an inner Earth?" you ask. Your voice sounds strange and hollow as you say the words.

The three adults nod. "It appears so, but they have still not made it work to go all the way inside," Harry says.

"Your parents were working there. They made great progress deciphering the transit mechanism and how it worked. We were trying to keep it secret from the central government. But word leaked," he adds.

"Why would the government be interested?" Peter asks.

"Because of where it leads, and what's inside," François comments, speaking for the first time. "We don't know exactly what they are after. But we do know they are desperate."

"The reason we were down there was to access the volcanic tube system. The whole thing came about when your father found the map vessel. It showed us where to look further." As Harry says this, he pulls out a picture of a large, amphora-shaped clay vessel. You recognize it. At least you recognize part of it.

"That's the shard!" Peter yells. "That's the same thing!"

"You mean this?" you ask, pulling the shard out of your backpack. Its familiar weight and shape is comforting in your hand.

"*Zut alors!*" François swears, reaching his hand out toward the shard. You pull it back quickly. "What's that doing here? I thought I had seen the last of that damn thing!"

"What do you mean?" Peter asks. "I found that out in the middle of the desert, not in the caverns. Fair and square."

The body language shifts and the adults are exchanging knowing looks.

"I need to take that shard, now!" François says, his eyes wide. "It has a tracking transponder hidden in it. That was why I threw it away. Harry can explain more. I need to get that thing out of here or we will all be captured! Harry and Maggie can explain, but you need to give me the shard!" he barks.

"What about my parents?"

"Schliemann arrested them," Harry replies, "and brought them here. To Carlsbad. They are there right now, I believe. At the site. Unless the first pod has departed."

"Departed for where?" you cry.

"For whatever lies inside," Maggie answers.

You give François the shard. It's like part of your soul goes with it. Even if it is contaminated with a transponder. It feels like your last link to your parents.

Harry rolls back the door of the storage unit, and François ducks out into the last rays of sunset. You see him run around the corner, before Harry slams the door shut again.

"We don't have much time," he says. "Trust François though; he'll give them a good chase. Other Gatekeepers will come and check out this location soon. They are nothing if not thorough. Anyway, there is one more piece of information you need before we go on the rescue mission for your parents tonight."

With those words Harry lifts a blanket off an old-style trunk with brass corners. It stands on its end. Harry swings the top open like a door. A blaze of white light stabs out as soon as the first crack appears. You shield your eyes.

"What the hell?" Peter cries. Dresdale flinches briefly. You are too stunned to say anything.

A glowing doll-sized figure steps out of the trunk. Its hands and face shine with a radiance that is much brighter than Harry's small lamp. It is wearing toddler's clothes, but its face is older looking. A soft fuzz of hair on its head cuts down on the glowing, but only a little bit.

"Hello." The figure's voice is light and high. It sounds a bit like singing.

"Schliemann may have gotten the lab, and a complete copy of the vessel maps, but he did not get to meet one of the Illuminated," Harry says, gesturing to the glowing being standing before you.

You think the Pooh Bear sneakers are a good touch. They light up too.

"Our friend here also needs to get into the lab complex. We have been planning a double mission of getting your parents and also helping Neila return to the inside. He is sick, and he needs to go home," Maggie explains.

"What's your name?" Dresdale asks, crouching down to talk to the Illuminated One. "I'm Dresdale."

A high pitched whistle is her answer. You have a hunch most of it is pitched above your hearing. "But you can call me Neila of the Illuminated. You will be coming with us to the inside?" The small figure turns to look at you.

"I don't know, maybe. I'd like to know my parents are actually headed inside. Where do you need to go?" you reply.

"You *have* to come," Neila says loudly, his face fierce in yours. Everyone starts. His small teeth are sharp. "You are the cup of the emerald. You are the child of the child. From above to deep inside."

"Listen, I don't know what you are talking about," you say. You look at Dresdale and Peter. "But I do know that I need to find my parents."

"I just want to find them," you add, looking at Maggie and Harry. "I just need to know they're okay."

"We don't have time for this discussion now. The Gatekeepers will be here any minute," Harry replies, pulling the door open again. "Are you coming with us? Otherwise I can give you a map of the complex if you want to try to find your parents on your own. In some ways a smaller group without baggage might be better. If you do decide to join us, you must do exactly as we say."

You don't know if he's talking about you or Neila being the baggage. You look at Dresdale and Peter.

If you choose to help Neila the Illuminated One and head into the Left-Hand Tunnel, turn to page 165.

If you decide to risk going after your parents by yourself with a map of the complex and the tunnel, turn to page 70.

"My Name Is Lucas Foren"

"My parents were headed to see Mr. Billings. Or at least that was their plan before they disappeared. I don't know why, but going to New York feels like the best call," you say, making your mind up as you speak. "Something about the way Billings was talking convinced me that going to Carlsbad is dangerous."

"So, what do we do then?" Peter asks. "We can't take the flyer to New York, we don't have the transportation controls."

"We take your car of course!" Dresdale says brightly.

"I love that car more than almost anything," replies Peter, "but I'm not sure she could make it the whole way. She is so old, I don't think we could find any replacement parts. And we don't have the travel docs."

"Billings said he would email them to me in the morning," you reply. "We shouldn't stay here tonight. My mom's email and Mr. Billings agreed on that point. It isn't safe here."

"Why don't we just drive through the night?" asks Peter with a grin. "I was planning on pulling an all-nighter for the trig test anyway."

"We don't have enough fuel," Dresdale points out.

"We should have some fuel in the garage," you tell her. "You know, for the lawnmower and stuff."

"What are we going to do about Tito?" Dresdale asks.

With your parents missing and possibly kidnapped, you forgot about Tito. "Take him with us?" you say, unsure.

"Gross!" says Peter. "Sorry, no way am I bringing a dead dog in my car."

"We can't just leave him here!" says Dresdale, punching Peter in the arm. He winces but does not say anything.

"No, Peter's right," you admit. "There's no sense bringing him with us, but you are right too, I can't just leave him like this."

"We could bury him in the garden," Peter suggests, crouching a bit to ward off any potential blows from Dresdale.

"That makes sense," says Dresdale. "The ground is soft, and he is little, so it shouldn't take much time."

"I'll do it," says Peter.

"No, it's okay," you say. "He was my mom's dog, and sort of my dog too. I'll take care of it. Can you two pack up anything you think we'll need? Just throw it in Peter's car. I'll go get the shovel and the fuel can. Let's try to be out of here in less than fifteen minutes."

Dresdale and Peter nod and silently go to work. From the light of the kitchen windows, you can see enough of the garden to pick out a good spot for Tito's grave. You choose a flat space between two sedum plants and start digging. Working quickly, you make a hole about two feet deep by one foot wide.

Hopefully coyotes won't dig him up; you don't have time to put him six feet under.

By the time you finish, you have started to warm up in the cold night air and are breathing hard. Dresdale and Peter load the car with your supplies. "Goodbye, Tito," you say. "You deserved better." Part of you wants to add "I deserve better!" but you stuff the self-pity for now.

"Hey, Peter! I told you to take things you thought we might need, not to loot the whole house!" you say, looking over his haul.

"You never know what you might need. Didn't the Boy Scouts say be prepared?" he responds.

"Look what happened to them," mutters Dresdale, shoving your old musty tent into Peter's trunk. "Did you, you know, bury him?"

"Yeah, let's go. I know it's risky, but let's see if we can get somewhere before dawn without the Gatekeepers finding us."

You drive through the night, but even when it is not your turn to drive, you can't sleep. Thoughts of the house, of Tito, and of your parents torment you. Toward dawn you come to a small town in western Tennessee. The roads have been in tough shape the whole way, and are getting worse. Peter's car bounces and makes a grinding noise every time you go over a bump. The morning sunrise is beautiful over the cornfields. The harvested fields look like strange cemeteries for armies of toy soldiers, with the cut stalks as rows of headstones.

"We shouldn't push our luck," you say. "Let's pull over, get something to eat and see if Billings has emailed the travel passes."

"Sounds good to me," Dresdale says. "I need to stretch. Besides, I should let my parents know we are all right."

"Are we?"

"Of course we are! We're going to find your parents and convince that stupid Alstone School that they were wrong to kick us out," she says. "You have to believe that, otherwise it will never happen!"

"I guess," you say. You are more shaken up than you care to admit.

Even a small town like Brownsville has an Internet café, so the three of you order coffees and log on. Mr. Billings did as he said, and you are able to print out your travel documents. By 9:30 you are back on the road. Peter sleeps in the back while Dresdale drives. Unfortunately Dresdale is unable to reach either her mom or dad . She leaves voicemails and sends them both email saying that she is safe with you. You feel guilty, because you aren't exactly sure that it's true.

"How were Billings and Rimy able to get travel docs so fast?" you ask Dresdale as you look out the window.

"I don't know," she says. "But add that to the list of unexplained mysteries. It's always taken us a much longer time to get clearances. When my parents took me to the Florida remnant, it took over a month to come through. My mom was freaking out that we wouldn't be able to go after Dad had already paid for the hotel, but we finally got it two days before the trip."

As you get closer to Nashville, you notice that there is more and more traffic. At first you figure that it's just because you are getting near a large city. However, soon the traffic comes to a complete standstill and you move ahead at a start, but mostly stop, pace.

"What's going on?" says Peter, yawning from the back of the car. "Have we gotten to New York yet?

"Sorry buddy," you say. "Looks like a traffic jam."

"I thought there weren't any traffic jams anymore?"

"Well, take a look out the window. Do you see all the cars backed up? I've been inching along now for over two hours while you snored in the back," Dresdale comments with the sharpness that comes from too little sleep and too much looking at the back of the same car in front of you.

Finally you move forward enough to see what is going on. The cars are being taken off the road and into a huge parking lot where the Gatekeepers are running a full inspection. This could be a disaster if you are on their list. You see lots of stressed-looking businesspeople arguing with bored Gatekeepers. Ominously, you see a long row of parked and empty cars and a longer row of people lining up at the back end of the parking lot.

"You made sure the papers were in order, right?" asks Peter as you get nearer to the makeshift screening booth.

"Yeah," you say, feeling nervous. "Here they are, check them out for yourself. It all looks okay to me."

"I trust you," he says defensively.

"Remember the story, we are meeting my parents in New York for a meeting with Mr. Billings and then going to see a show. They had to travel ahead of us."

"Papers, please," says the bored Gatekeeper when it is your

turn. Dresdale hands him the papers and you wait in silence as he looks them over. He hums while he shuffles through the papers and makes notes on them. After more than five minutes of humming and looking, you want to tell him to shut up, but you restrain yourself. You have learned that it is best not to make enemies of civil servants, especially when they can block you from what you want.

"Looks like there's a problem here," he says finally, after tapping on his wrist computer for a while more. "These papers are only valid if there is an adult along. None of you have reached your majority, correct?"

"Please, sir, we just need to get to New York to meet up with my parents," you plead. Your stomach, already upset about getting kicked out of school and finding your parents missing or kidnapped, clenches so much that you taste bile in the back of your throat.

The Gatekeeper officer looks up from the papers and glares at the three of you. "Have any of you three reached your majority, and more importantly, do you have proof to that effect?"

"No, sir, but we are just trying to get to New York," says Dresdale, using her best nonthreatening and sweet voice. "Could you please just let us go?"

"That's not my job," he says with a smile. "Get out of the car. You need to have your claim seen by a supervisor. I guess that you won't get clearance."

"Isn't there some way we could just take care of this now?" says Peter. "You know, like if you could take care of it, and we, well, we could take care of you?"

"Are you offering me a bribe?" asks the Gatekeeper. The smile is gone. "Because if you are, that is a federal felony punishable by up to five years in prison."

"No, sir!" says Peter hurriedly. "That's not what I meant!"

"Like I said, get out of the car. Now!"

The Gatekeeper hands you a slip of paper and tells you to report to the hearings court in the morning. "Just be lucky that I didn't put you into protective custody like those poor fools over there," he says, pointing to the long line of people on the far side of the parking lot. "You don't want to go where they are going. I am doing you a real favor here. Don't forget it."

Peter grimaces when he hands over the keys. You pat his shoulder in understanding. All you take are your backpacks.

"Now what?" you ask no one in particular.

"We get out of here before they change their minds and put us in protective custody," Dresdale says firmly. She puts her words into action and walks away from the clogged parking lot and its line of desperate looking people.

The road leads toward the nearest town. You are amazed by how few cars are on the streets after the blockade. Peter puts his thumb out to hitch a ride, but the drivers look away and speed by. Nobody wants to be involved. People are paralyzed by fear of the Gatekeepers.

"I don't blame them," says Peter. "I wouldn't pick us up either. People want to avoid trouble these days."

Exhausted after all the events of the past day, you wander in a haze, letting Peter and Dresdale take the lead. Later, you come to a small roadside restaurant called Pixel's Café. Human fuel is what you need. Peter and you order the chili con carne, while Dresdale gets a pot of strong tea and the vegetarian chili. Peter tries to order a beer, but the waitress just looks at him and laughs, saying, "you might be old enough for root beer, son."

"What are we going to do! How can we get to New York without my car?" Peter asks in frustration.

"Excuse me," says a goateed man reading his tablet notebook at the table next to yours. "I happened to overhear you just now. I may be able to help." Middle-aged, he has dark hair cut short, and he is wearing worker's overalls. He looks strong, with large hands, and his eyes are smiling along with his mouth.

"You can get my car back?" says Peter with desperate hope in his voice.

"Unfortunately I can't do that," says the man. "But I'm going to New York, or near enough, anyways, I would be happy to take the three of you along. For some consideration."

"What about my friend's car?" you ask. "They said to go to the hearing tomorrow and we might get it back."

The man at the table laughs, and you see that his teeth are small and perfect. "That would be truly amazing. I couldn't help but overhear your conversation. That Gatekeeper did do you all a huge favor. Give up on seeing your car ever again and be thankful they didn't take you all to Iowa City. Things have been getting too hot around here. The Quebec insurgency has been making gains up north and they're worried that this area is the next big target. Everyone is nervous about the FFA, but they can't talk about it on the official news stations."

"How much?" you ask.

"A thousand sounds about right. My name is Lucas Foren. Pleased to meet you," he says, scooting his chair closer and extending his hand.

"A thousand dollars? Just to get to New York?" you ask, incredulous.

Turn to page 72.

Willow

My mom told me to go see Uncle Harry, whoever he is, so that's what I'm going to do. Besides, flying sounds a lot easier than trying to get to New York in your jalopy. No offense, Peter."

"None taken. I'm not sure she could make it the whole way myself," he replies. "Let's go."

Peter gets food from the kitchen, while you and Dresdale go to the garage and unwrap the flyer. It's the size and shape of a small car and it looks pretty inconspicuous under its blue tarp. Dark green paint glints on the pointed shape of the flyer's nose after you uncover it. Your pulse quickens just looking at it; you aren't quite as easy about flying it as you said.

You load as much food and supplies as you can in the flyer's tiny hatches. Your parents were supposed to return the flyer after the dig, but they never did. You asked them why, and they always gave you sideways answers. Almost nobody was allowed flyers anymore. The Gatekeepers liked keeping people from moving around too easily.

"Where are we gonna get fuel?" asks Peter as you open the workshop garage, move ten layers of junk, and remove the tarp covering the flyer. "No one is supposed to have one."

"This thing is pretty amazing," you say while removing the tarp and checking the exterior of the flyer. "It sips like a hummingbird from regular synth-fuel. Push comes to shove, it can run on ethanol or other available energy sources. Besides, its flying range is over a thousand miles and we aren't that far from Carlsbad."

"You do know how to fly this thing?" Dresdale queries doubtfully.

"Yeah, my dad showed me how to fly it to shut me up once I started asking too many questions about it. Mom and dad always acted sort of embarrassed that they had it."

"I think it's cool. Will you let me fly it?"

"Sure, Peter, but let's see if we can get it going first."

Your head spins with all the events of the day, but doing something, anything, seems to help shore up the wall of anxiety that threatens to crush you. Once the flyer is in the air, you skim low over the treetops of the vast forests near your home. The auto-pilot does most of the work, keeping you at a safe fifty-foot clearance of all obstacles while using a satellite guidance and map system to plot the course. A low swishing sound is the only noise that the flyer makes as it whirs through the darkness. You keep the lights off.

You fly through the night, looking at the ground below. Dim light from a crescent moon gives everything a silvery tint. A tint of unreality, just like the day that you are still enduring. Where are your parents? Are they all right? Should you have gone to New York City instead? Somehow the activity of flying helps you to avoid screaming or curling up into a ball on the floor. That and the large travel mug of coffee that Peter handed you. You aren't sure how he was able to pack up so much stuff so quickly and make three cups of coffee all at the same time, but you appreciate it.

"You two are the best friends anyone could ever ask for," you say, meaning it. "This is all my fault. Without me, they would have left you guys alone."

"Hey, I was the one who found the shard. Remember?" Peter says from the backseat. His voice is muffled by the fact that his knees are almost touching his face.

"Thanks, that's nice," says Dresdale. "You too, but you do know that I was almost asleep? Let's talk about it in the morning."

"Sorry," you say. "What do you think we should do about

flying during the day though? Dawn is only a couple of hours away."

"We're pushing our luck right now. Flying during the day would be stupid," Peter says. "Even if the flyer has the right codes, they are rare enough that someone would call the Gatekeepers. People are paranoid."

"I buy that. So, where do we hide the flyer?"

"I packed the tarp, so we could just pretend to be camping. Hey, Dresdale, wake up! Keep an eye open up there for someplace where we can hide this thing during the day. Try and make it as out-of-the-way as possible."

Both of you keep your eyes open for a likely spot to hide the flyer, but it is Peter, from the back, who spots the downed tree by the moonlit sliver of silver river.

"There it is guys! Let's take a look!" he says, as excited as a first grader on a field trip. You smile for a brief moment before setting the flyer into hover mode and slowly lowering it by the downed tree. You land in a clearing to the south of the tree. Dawn's red light gives the dried leaves of the weeping willow a sinister, bloody look. You hope that is just your tired brain looking for trouble.

You move the flyer under the hanging leaves and branches of the dead tree. The branches are brittle but serve to hide the flyer completely from view.

"Looks like a big storm took this old tree down," says Peter, examining the jagged stump where the massive tree had broken.

As soon as the flyer is stowed under the tree, Dresdale takes a blanket and lies down under its left wing. But you are too jazzed up to sleep, even though you are exhausted, so you and

Peter decide to explore your surroundings. All you find are some fields of wheat beyond the copse of trees. The wheat is ripe and ready for the harvest. You think about bread and decide to go back, but as you turn away from the field, you see a burst of light.

"Did you see that?" you ask Peter.

"See what?" says Peter, heading back to the river bank.

"That flash, over on the other side of the field!"

"Nope, I didn't see anything. Let's grab some food and get some sleep," says Peter.

"It was really bright, almost like a mini-sun," you explain. "Do you want to go take a look?"

"Not really," he says with a huge yawn. "I'm exhausted. Come on."

If you choose to try to explore the brilliant flash of light alone, turn to page 97.

If you realize that you are too tired to take a look and go get some sleep instead, go on to the next page.

"Uncle" Harry

You head back to your camp site. Lying under the canopy of the dead willow branches, you feel safe, even though your whole world has changed dramatically in less than twenty-four hours. Your mind swirls like the nearby river. You fall asleep thinking about all the strange events that have happened so quickly.

You wake up hot and alone. A mosquito has dined on your left cheek. Where are you? Your stomach clenches as reality sinks in. You move through the dead willow branches. You spot your friends down at the bank of the river. Peter has a wide smile, and a stick and a line in the brown and swirly water. It's like a movie set.

"Good afternoon, sleepyhead," Dresdale says.

"Well, if it isn't Huck and Tom! Don't you two have a fence to paint?" you say with forced cheeriness. "I don't think you are going to catch anything in this river."

"Open your eyes, doubters, and you will see the truth!" Peter replies, picking up a large fish from the ground. Its mouth gapes open at you. "Looks like this poor fellow failed his trig test!"

If the day before had not happened, you would have considered the day by the river with Peter and Dresdale one of the best of your life. The three of you swim in the swift water, eat catfish cooked on sticks, and sit in the warm sun. The day before did happen, though, and the dark cloud of your parents being gone hangs over you and drains the day of its joy.

"What really happened back at the Discipline Board?" says Dresdale after you finish the catfish and the potato chips that Peter had taken from your kitchen. "Why did they roll over for this Schliemann character?"

"I've been thinking about that. He obviously has power. Something is going on," Peter agrees.

"I think it's a part of the whole governmental power struggle," you say. "Headmaster Cummings basically said as much in the meeting."

"You mean with the FFA and the insurgency?" Dresdale asks.

"What does a government power struggle have to do with an ancient pot? Remember he said the shard was part of some pot?" Peter adds.

You shrug because you don't have any easy answers. "I wish my parents had told me that they had been replaced by that guy! If we hadn't seen that news article about the volcanic explosions, we still wouldn't even know that he had taken over the Carlsbad expedition."

"The question is why Carlsbad?" asks Dresdale. "We were all there. Did you ever see any reason why someone inside the government would want to control it?"

"Remember the Left-Hand Tunnel area?" you say. "How it was roped off for instability? I saw people coming from there more than once."

"So did I," says Peter. "One time I tried to get in there to look around and someone stopped me. I always thought they found something, but what?"

"Peter, where were you exactly, when you found the shard?" Dresdale asks.

"Actually not far from there," Peter answers. "I was bushwacking near the Muir trailhead. Maybe 2000 feet from the Left-Hand Tunnel."

"Humor me on this," Dresdale says. "I know we've looked at it a million times. But let's look again."

You produce the shard from your jacket. Everything is familiar after months of analyzing it, but now that it has added importance, you try to view the shard in a new light. It might be the key to finding your parents. About the size of your hand, and curved slightly, as if part of some vessel, it has marks in an unknown language. The writing looks tantalizingly like it might be pictographic, but in a highly stylized way. The picture fragment is of a humanoid figure holding up something above its head, but that part is broken off, so you can't see it. None of the features are realistic, but it is done in such a modern way you can see why you all thought it might just be some funky pattern on a series of dish plates. That was before you had positively dated it to over 700 years old. You keep looking, but you don't see anything new.

"If this is the answer to our problems, I don't see it," you say with the despair that threatens you. "I should just throw it away!"

"Don't do that! Here, give it to me. I'll keep it for you," Dresdale says. "Who knows how it might help us? But let's get back on track. We're going to Carlsbad to see Uncle Harry at the local Federal Historical Accuracy Board? You've never met the guy, and he's supposed to be your uncle? Anyway, how do we get into town and down there without getting spotted? Why can't we just call him?"

"All phone calls are tapped," you explain. "That's why they outlawed cell phones. It's too hard to track people with cells. They just swap them around."

"Yeah, I know that, but they can't monitor every call! Just the important ones."

"Well, my mom's email said not to call."

"We could park the flyer near the junkyard on the western outskirts and walk into town," offers Peter. "You know, put the tarp over it and maybe people will think it is junk."

"Maybe, but let's see if we come up with anything better. We are about halfway there. I think we are on a tributary of the Mississippi. The GPS route finder didn't have the river listed, but it looks pretty big to me."

A burnt orange sunset arrives. All three of you are anxious to leave, but when you push the flyer out from under the branches what you really feel like is getting back inside to go to sleep. Once you get into the air, though, you feel better. Peter is in the front seat so he watches how you control the flyer. It's a pretty basic yoke system with safety overrides. Anytime you put the aircraft in a dangerous attitude, it gently straightens the stick out by itself. Still, it does take some skill and time to get the hang of.

"Fasten your seat belts, ladies and gentlemen! There's a big patch of turbulence coming up!"

"Oh no, here come a stream of bad captain jokes," moans Dresdale from the back as Peter takes the stick and lifts off from the field that you landed in. You clutch the armrest of your chair as Peter sends you into a sharp banking roll. He carefully tests the machine to see how fast, slow, steep, and quickly it will turn and fly. You felt a lot safer when you were doing the flying.

"I think you should learn how to fly, too," says Peter to Dresdale after he had been flying for a couple of hours.

"Okay," says Dresdale. "May as well have all of us know how to use this thing."

Dresdale masters the flyer the fastest of you all, and she flies you over the desert leading toward Carlsbad. Even with stopping to change flyers and having them learn on the job, you still manage to come within sight of the city's outskirts before dawn. You land in the desert near the junkyard and then the three of you push the flyer closer to its corrugated iron fence.

Big boulders and scrub break up the landscape around you, and you see bits of random junk beyond the big fence, but you think the flyer sticks out even with the tarp completely covering it.

"It will just have to do," says Dresdale as the three of you look at the covered flyer in the orange glow of the desert sunrise. "Hopefully for just a few hours, anyway."

"Let's get going to town. It's cold." You shiver in the

morning air involuntarily.

The walk to town only takes about an hour. The Federal Historical Accuracy Board office doesn't open until 9 AM, so the three of you stop and get breakfast at a greasy spoon diner. You wash up as best you can in the bathroom, but Peter still tells you that your hair looks like a sick hedgehog. You would like to tell him the same, but he somehow looks well-groomed and fresh.

"Time to go meet Uncle Harry!" says Dresdale brightly as the hour strikes. You hope that he can lead you to your parents. Or at least help you in some way.

The FHAB office is in a low slung, gray building that looks like a flat worm trying to bury itself to get away from the morning sun. It is nothing special, just a building, but you have a feeling of fear mixed with excitement as you get closer. Peter and Dresdale wait across the street. They are pretending to be reading the newspaper on a park bench, but they are both watching you too much for their ruse to be believable. Maybe you are just paranoid.

"May I help you?" asks the man behind the desk in the lobby of the FHAB building. He is wearing a cap and has a big ID badge pinned to his white shirt.

"Yeah, I'm, uh, here to see Harry Turner. He's in suite 11B."

"Don't you mean suite B11? Do you have an appointment?"

"Yeah, B11, and, no, uh, he's my uncle. Can you just tell him I'm here?"

The receptionist holds his hand over his mouth while he makes the call to Uncle Harry, so you can't hear what they say.

"Wait there on the couch. He'll be out here to see you soon," he says.

Each time the door opens, you look up expectantly, but no one so much as glances at you as they scurry across the lobby and out into the bright day. After ten long minutes, the door opens. A middle-aged, gray-haired man with glasses comes out and looks around the lobby. He's sweating, even though the air conditioning is going full blast.

"Ah, there you are!" he says loudly and heartily, as if on-stage. "Your mother didn't tell me you had grown so much!"

"Uncle Harry," you say, holding out your hand. "Thank you so much for seeing me. I really need your help. My mom said to ask you…"

"Not here, not here, not now!" he says, interrupting you by laughing loudly. "I'm swamped, just swamped with work today, so I thought you could come by my house after work. We can talk then!"

"Can't we just talk now?" you say. "I've come a long way."

"Don't I know it! Don't I know it! When your mom told me you were coming here on your fall break, I said to her wow, that's a long way to come, just to see old Uncle Harry, but she said you really needed to talk to me. Look, I know you want to hear about all my old crazy adventures in the FHAB, but I really can't right now!"

As he says the last words, he reaches out, grabs your forearm, squeezes it hard, and looks you in the eye. Putting aside your fear, need and disappointment, you take the hint.

"Great, no problem. I'll meet you at your house after work. What time?"

"Here, let me give you the directions. Five-thirty should be fine," he says as he takes out a pad of paper and starts writing. You wonder how many people carry a pad and pen these days. Certainly not many. "Remember, five-thirty at my house!"

With that he turns, swipes his ID card against the reader and goes back to his office. He doesn't look back.

You read the piece of paper as you walk out the door into the bright sunshine. All it says is an address and a name "U-Stor-It, unit 34, 285 Pinon Street." Wherever it is, it does not sound like his home address.

Peter and Dresdale are visibly excited. Their newspapers lie forgotten on the bench next to them.

"Cool it, guys," you mouth at them as you cross the street. They don't hear you and head toward you in a rush.

"What happened? Did you see Uncle Harry? What did he say?"

"Let's get out of here," you say, grabbing the two of them by the arms and walking down the street. A black car parked across from the FHAB building pulls out into traffic. Just to be safe, you cut down one of the side streets. Away from the main street, Carlsbad rapidly loses its crowds. Few people and fewer cars are on the street in just a hundred feet. *"What did he say?"* Dresdale fumes under her breath as you continue to push her and Peter in front of you. "Stop grabbing me, too! You are such a control freak! Just tell us what happened. No one is around."

You realize this is true, so you let go of their arms and slow down a bit. "Sorry, just the whole thing was really freaky. We were pretending to know each other, but we had never seen each other before. It seemed fake, but scary. He seemed scared.

He told me he couldn't talk and to meet me at his house after work, but he wrote something different on this piece of paper," you say, handing the paper to Dresdale. "I don't mean to keep you guys out of the loop, but I don't know anything myself."

You look over your shoulder and your heart starts to race. The back car from the FHAB building is behind you.

Black car. BLACK CAR! You don't know how, but you know for sure that the car behind you is danger times trouble. You look around quickly. While you were talking to the other two, you had started passing a long, chain-link fence. You are in the middle of the fence. The black car is getting close. Sweat streams into your eyes. The day has become hot.

"Can you guys jump over that fence?"

"Yeah. Why?"

"I think that car is coming after us," you say. "I think we need to get away."

"We could try and run around the corner instead. You sure that car is after us?"

"No, but I don't think we can take the chance, we need to do something!" As you say this, the black car pulls onto the sidewalk in front of you, the right rear door opens and a man dressed in a black suit yells out. "Get in the car! Now!"

Getting in the car is not even an option. You need to do something, and do it now.

If you choose to jump the fence to get away, turn to page 31.

If you decide to turn around and run back the way you came, turn to page 76.

"Thanks, but No Thanks"

I am sorry, but I have to find my parents," you explain, turning to face Durno and Sublimas-Chaeko and giving them a smile. "I am humbled by your offer of the Emerald Ritual, but I cannot accept it." You add a small bow for good measure.

You feel your heart thumping in your chest as your response is translated into Lemurian. Sublimas-Chaeko looks at you, and you try to meet his stare straight on, but you blink without meaning to. He sniffs the air and turns his head away from you.

"This is a tragic day," Durno says quietly. You can't tell if he was talking to Rimy or just to himself. "We didn't have an Emerald Channel before, so we can't miss what we never had."

"I was hoping you'd say yes, but it's okay that you chickened out. I'll still be your friend," Dresdale says. You can't tell if she is joking or not. "The ritual sounded pretty cool. I would have liked to have seen it."

"Don't listen to her. She's just jealous that they didn't pick her."

"Thanks, but no thanks!"

Dres rolls her eyes..

"Come on, guys, I feel bad enough without you rubbing it in," you say, moving toward the door. No one looks you in the eye, and the dinner that was in full swing mere moments ago is over.

Rimy is in your room. He has packed up all your gear.

"We have to go now," says Rimy as calmly as if he were asking for the sugar for his tea. "Durno says that an attack is expected here in the next few days. Whether that is true or not, they have asked us to depart."

"Right now?" says Peter. "I am so beat I am sure I dreamed you telling us we have to go tonight. Right?"

"No, you did not dream it, Peter. We have a long journey in front of us. Complaining uses energy. Save that energy for your hiking. And be thankful they are giving us Durno as a guide," Rimy answers.

The Lemurian encampment seems empty as you leave. You think you see Sublimas looking out of a window, but when you glance back the figure is gone.

Red light streams over the surface of the inner world. You, Dresdale, and Peter follow in Rimy's path. At first you climb steeply. You pause for a moment as you get to the top of a jagged red cliff. The inner sea stretches a long way, and your brain struggles to accept the image coming to you from your eyes. Instead of the horizon line cutting off your view, you can see more of the sea as it stretches upwards. Above you, the sun is just a tiny speck of burning brightness, surrounded by a reddish mist of clouds.

"It was not like this always," says Durno as he comes to

hurry you along. "Keep moving, we need to hurry."

"Okay, I'll come," you say. "But can you tell me more about your inner world?"

"When my father was little," he begins, after making sure that you are moving forward at an acceptable pace. "The sun was not so big, or so bright. Most of the land was barren, with little light or water. Rain was rare, and the Blood Red Sea was saltier, and lower. Much has changed. Keep moving."

You travel to the regional capital, in search of information about your parents. "Durno thinks that's our best chance of learning something," Rimy explains. The journey takes days. You stop at food caches to replenish supplies, but you see no one en route. Three days and quasi-nights after departing the first encampment, you crest a hill and look down on a small town. Durno frowns.

"There should be smoke. From cookfires," he states tersely. "Its absence makes me keen."

Durno takes off at a trot, and the four of your try to follow. Your mountain trail feeds into a road paved with cobblestones. Durno is now far ahead, running.

You finally reach the Arcata city gates. Durno stands quietly, tears streaming down his face.

"There has been an evacuation," he whispers. "This cannot be good."

"I think I hear someone crying," Dresdale says. She darts forward, looking.

You follow and turn a corner on to a town square. A young girl, covered in soot, runs toward you sobbing.

"What is she saying?" you ask. She jumps into Durno's

grasp and throws her small arms around him.

Durno listens as the young girl speaks haltingly.

He looks slowly to you as she speaks.

"Strangers came. They ordered the men into the woods. She thinks they were shot. And the women and children were forced to march to the capital."

Durno asks a few questions.

"She says some of the strangers were from your people, from the outer Earth," he continues.

You hold out a photo of your mom and dad in your wallet.

"Did you see these people?" you ask.

"Yes, they were in the lead," Durno translates.

Plaster explodes above your head. Your cheek is a small flower of pain. Durno lies at your feet. He is not moving.

"Come on! Grab him, we need to get out of here!"

Please go to page 29 of The Golden Path
Volume II: Burned By The Inner Sun

Family First

I'll take my chances alone. I'm so sorry, but I...I just think I'll have a better chance of helping my parents. Whatever has happened to them," you say.

Harry exchanges a glance with Maggie Carlson, and nods. He opens a small satchel and pulls out a carefully folded paper.

"This is the most up to date map we have. With the current security in place. Which has increased substantially since last summer."

You unfold the paper and take a quick look.

"We need to leave this place. We can drop you on the way," Maggie says.

"Take this walkie-talkie, they're illegal to own, but if you need help, we'll do what we can."

"Thanks," you say, meaning it.

They drive toward the caves and drop you off at a motel

near town's edge. All three of you are exhausted, and you have agreed you need a night's sleep and time to make a plan.

"First shower!" Dresdale calls. She takes a short one, but Peter uses almost all the hot water. You are shivering from the cold water and covered with soap when the Gatekeepers barge into the bathroom. They throw a towel at you and escort you out.

"Help us!" Peter yells into the walkie-talkie as two Gatekeepers grab him.

By the time the FFA members respond to your SOS, you are gone and there is no trace of you left at the motel.

You are one of the lucky ones. The Gatekeepers process you as runaways. After three years in a Juvenile Detention center, they let you go. Peter is also released, or so you learn, as he is kept at a different facility.

You never see Dresdale or your parents again.

The End

Continued from page 51

"Well, you're welcome to try and get there yourself. Trust me, you will need my help. I have the proper papers to get through. Very few others can say the same and be telling the truth." With that he goes back to sipping his beer and reading his tablet, but then he looks back up at you and says. "I'll be leaving in about five minutes, so let me know if you are interested before then."

"I think we should try and get my car back," whispers Peter. "How can we trust this guy? What if he is some sort of creep? Besides, we don't have a thousand dollars!"

"Normally I would completely agree with you," Dresdale whispers. "But right now we're desperate. That scene back in the parking lot was weird. Even if he is a creep, I think he is probably right about our chances of getting your car back." She pauses to let the reality sink and adds, "Sorry, Peter."

If you decide to travel with Lucas Foren to New York, turn to page 78.

If you decide to risk attending the hearing to try to get Peter's car back, turn to page 88.

A Darkness in the Night

MOOSE! Moose! *Moose!*" you yell as you put your hands over your ears and move forward into a crouch. You hear Lucas swearing.

"Watch out!"

Tires squeal as Foren jams on the brakes and swerves out of the way of the moose. You can't see anything with your head between your knees, but you know immediately when impact occurs. Glass shatters all over your body, and you hear high- and low-pitched noises from the twisting metal of the front of the van.

Something wet, soft, and smelly crashes into your head, but stops before it can crush you. You feel the muscles of the moose's leg and hind quarters as it struggles out of the wreckage. As soon as it is gone, you sit up and look around.

"Are you all right?" Lucas asks. He is pale and shaking.

"I don't know," you answer. The windshield is in small pieces all around you, and the rain is falling on your face. You look into the night. The moose is standing on the side of the road and gingerly stretching its injured leg. He shakes his head and gives a loud bellow of pain. Even in the dark, you can see that his rack of antlers is enormous. He tries a few steps and almost falls. Then you start to come out of the immediate shock of the crash: *Peter and Dresdale!*

You try to unbuckle your seat belt, but it is jammed.

"Lucas!! Check on Peter and Dresdale! I can't get out of this thing."

"Okay!" Lucas looks very dazed, but he manages to get up and go in the back. Gear is strewn about in back of the van, and all you can see is one corner. You can see Peter's leg. It's not moving. You tug frantically at your seatbelt, but it doesn't give.

"Dresdale's breathing! She's knocked out, but breathing," Lucas yells from the back.

"What about Peter?" Your voice is hoarse with strain and fear.

"I think he's breathing. Yes, he is. Ohh, man! Hold on! His leg is twisted really badly."

"Wha, wha happen'?" Peter mumbles. "ARRAR-RRRRRRRHHH!"

You waited for two hours before the ambulance was able to get to you. During that time, you splinted and elevated Peter's broken leg. Lucas used the first aid kit to give him some ibuprofen and then iced him down. Dresdale woke up, but had to remain lying down due to her concussion.

You are in the emergency room when the Gatekeepers rush into your examination room. They merely rip the curtain away and stand there in the hospital with their guns drawn and rain glistening on their armor. They take you and no one says a word.

The End

The Final Chase

Moving without thinking, you turn around and run toward the corner. Peter and Dresdale follow. All three of you are good, strong runners and you make good time. You are almost at the end of the block when another large black car pulls up in front of you.

Looking over your shoulder, you see two big men in dark suits approaching rapidly. Their shoes make loud slapping sounds as they hit the sidewalk. People are getting out of the car in front of you. You run into the street. There are no cars around and no people.

Someone tackles you from behind, and you fall onto the pavement face first.

CARLSBAD COURIER

OCTOBER 23 CARLSBAD, NM

EXPELLED STUDENTS MISSING

BY ALBERTO GOMEZ

Three expelled minor-aged students from the prestigious Alstone boarding school, Peter Kim, Dresdale Hamilton and _________ ________, have been reported missing. They were last seen visiting Mr. Harry Turner of the Federal Historical Accuracy Board on October 18th. Mr. Turner has been taken in for questioning, but no known relationship between Mr. Turner and the young adults has been disclosed. Somehow the expelled students managed to travel over 1,000 miles in less than two days from their school to Carlsbad, NM. It is not known why the students came to the Carlsbad area. If anyone has any information about the current whereabouts of any of these three, please contact your local Gatekeepers office, or me, at Alberto_Gomez@carlsbad courier.us&p.newspaper

The End

New York Swansong

"Can we talk this over a little bit, Lucas? We don't have enough money right now to pay a thousand dollars to get to New York," you begin.

"That's the price," he says. "I have to cover my costs. Getting the clearances is becoming harder every day. You can't trust anyone."

"We just don't have it. All we have is $428 in cash."

"Can you get more?" Foren asks, leaning forward and stashing his tablet in his bag. "I could work something out then."

"Well, we are going to see my parent's financial adviser. He'll give me money, but maybe not the whole six hundred."

"If you can't pay up front, the total would be an additional eight hundred," Foren replies. "Don't worry though. I'm more than worth it. You wouldn't stand a chance of getting there without my help. Give me the four hundred now and we'll put the eight hundred for you to pay when we get to New York.

We should go now. Finish up your meal. To show you I'm not such a bad guy, I'll even pay for it."

With that, Lucas Foren gives a sharp laugh and lays down a bill to pay the check. The three of you follow him outside into the hot air of the fall day. You hope that you are not making a mistake.

"Over here," says Foren, pointing to the parking lot behind Pixel's Café. "It might be a bit cramped in the back, I have a lot of gear."

"Hey, that's a Gatekeeper cruiser!" Peter exclaims. The blue and white vehicle is ominous. "How did you get that? You're not part of the Gatekeepers are you?"

Foren laughs again; he seems to do it a lot. "No, but I am in charge of Metropolitan vehicle maintenance for the city of Brooklyn. We deal with thousands of cars, busses, and flyers each year. If you look closely, you'll see that this isn't a standard officer's cruiser, but an administrative vehicle. Notice that there aren't any lights or anything. But it is still helpful getting people out of my way on the road. No one wants to mess with the Gatekeepers these days."

You notice that he doesn't laugh when he says that.

"If you're in charge of maintenance, why do you need to get money from people like us?" says Dresdale challengingly as she gets in the car.

"You'd be surprised how little we civil servants are paid," says Foren as he starts the cruiser. It purrs to life with a low and powerful sound. "Anyway, I'm not really doing it for the money. I'm trying to help you. But you do still have to pay me.

Speaking of which, I believe the first four hundred is due now."

You get the money from Peter and Dresdale and hand it over to Foren. You feel even more vulnerable now than you did before. Nothing like being penniless to make the world seem more frightening, and it was doing a pretty good job of that before.

"Thanks," says Foren, putting the money into his pocket after counting it with one hand while driving. "Now, just settle back and enjoy the ride. If all goes well we should be there by tomorrow morning."

"What is all this junk, anyway?" asks Peter from the backseat. He is wedged in between odd pieces of machinery and parts.

"I told you I was head of vehicle maintenance. I had to come down here to pick up some parts."

"Couldn't you have brought a van or a truck?" Peter asks.

"Just relax," says Foren. He puts his foot down on the pedal and the car jumps forward.

You shift items out of your way and make a little space for yourself and Peter in the back. Very soon, you are both asleep, but before you drift off, you notice that Dresdale is staying awake. She is probably right to stay alert, but you are too tired to care anymore.

You wake up when you get to another roadblock checkpoint.

"Papers, sir," says the Gatekeeper. But he hardly glances at them before waving you through and wishing you a good trip. "This job has its perks," Foren says as he speeds away from the roadblock and its long line of cars still waiting to be processed.

Later, Foren stops and gets fuel. "You'll have to add that to the bill," you tell Foren sourly as he pays for the fuel and junk food. He laughs in reply.

"Don't you need to sleep?" you ask Foren. The sky is lightening to gray outside your window. It's nearly dawn.

"Nah," he says. "I'll catch up later. I need to get these parts to the garage, and then I have a few days off. I can catch up then. Normally I don't do the donkey work myself, but this was a rush mission. We have three Gatekeeper flyers that are grounded until we get these back to the shop. The mayor has his shorts in a knot because we need those flyers for some big shot who is coming to town."

He turns in his seat and looks at you directly.

"So, why are the three of you on the run?" he asks.

"We're not," you say defensively. "We just need help getting to New York. We'll meet up with my parents and then things will be fine."

"Okay, you don't have to tell me. Anyway, I'm going to go straight to the garage in Brooklyn. It is on high ground and not flooded, but you can catch a gondola-taxi or a ferry into Manhattan from there. You ever seen the Big Apple?"

"No," you answer. "But I've seen pictures."

"Well, get ready. It was a tough town before the flooding, but now all of the rats had to come out of the tunnels and move into the higher floors. Only the strong made it. Everyone else either moved or drowned."

"Were you alive when the big wave hit?" asks Dresdale. She looks exhausted, but you decide not to tell her that.

"Yeah, but I was just a little kid. The water had been creeping up for years before the tsunami came. Even so I don't think anyone was really ready for the big wave. Of course we knew that the Azores shelf had fallen, so most people had time to get out of the city and away to higher ground, but it was still amazing to see what a single wave could do. Skyscrapers fell down, fires broke out in ones that didn't get smashed. Tons of people who refused to leave died in their apartments. It was chaos."

"Did you see the wave?"

"Nah, my mom had us up in the Catskills with a cousin. But when we came back you wouldn't recognize the place. Junk and mud were everywhere. I never thought it would get rebuilt, but humans are stupid that way I guess. It isn't the same though." He notices something and looks up. "We're almost there. Take a look outside the right window and you can see the sun coming up over Manhattan. Still a beautiful sight."

From the almost deserted elevated highway, you see the sun shining red and orange among the towers that still reach for the sky. The water that lies between them is also red and orange from the reflected glow. It all looks unreal, like a painting from a book.

"Pretty crazy, huh!" says Peter. "Look at all the boats between the buildings, they look like water bugs skimming across a pond."

"Very poetic, Peter," says Dresdale. You can't tell if she is being sarcastic or not. "Where are we supposed to meet Mr. Billings?"

"His office is right off Central Pond, on the Upper East side," you answer.

"Should be easy to get there," says Lucas Foren. "Even though there are a lot fewer people living or commuting to the sunken island, it's still the center of business for the East coast. Here we are."

Foren pulls the cruiser into a large garage and lets you out. All around you, you see people working on various official-looking cars, buses, vans, and flyers. Foren talks to a couple of people and guides you to the water taxi stand. "Here's fifty to get you into the city," he says, handing you a crumpled bill. "Don't worry, I'll add it to your bill."

"How do you know we'll come back to pay you?" says Dresdale challengingly.

"I don't, but you have to take chances sometimes. Look, I could have you give me all your stuff until you come back, but what am I going to do with bookbags and dirty clothes?" he replies with a wink.

This time when he laughs, you can't help but laugh with him. You don't know how or when it happened, but sometime during the car trip with Lucas Foren, you have come to like and trust him.

"Let's go meet Preston Billings." says Dresdale brightly. "Maybe our luck is turning!"

"Let's hope so," says Peter. "I still miss my car. I can't believe they just took it like that."

"Believe it," you say. "It's gone."

The water taxi picks you up at a makeshift dock down the street from the garage and ferries you across the wide East River and into the dark canyons of the drowned city.

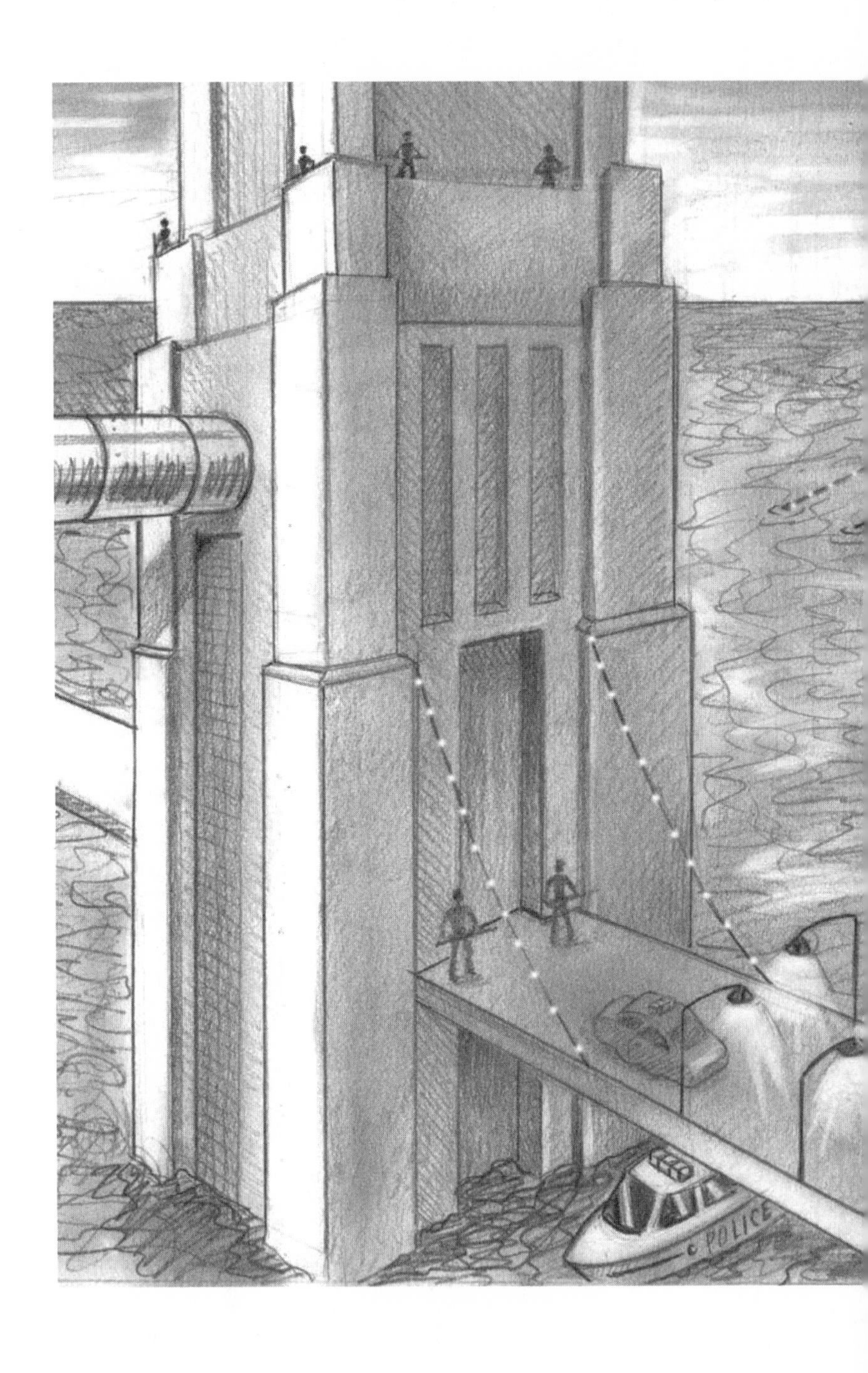
POLICE

"Hey, look," says Peter, pointing. "There's the Brooklyn Bridge! And it looks like there are trucks on it. How can people still drive into the city if it is under water?"

"Well, most of the city is under about twenty-five feet of water," explains the water taxi captain as he steers his boat among other boats and the stray piece of flotsam. "But the bridge and the elevated highways survived mostly intact. Or at least enough to be repaired. But they are just used for delivering stuff now. All of the traffic is by boat in the city proper."

"Is it always so stinky?" asks Dresdale "I don't mean to be rude . . ."

No worries," the captain says, "but, no, it isn't always so stinky. Just sometimes when the tide comes in the wrong way or an algae bloom gets settled in. Some people wanted to rename the city New Venice, but that never stuck."

The waves splash against the buildings as you get deeper into the old and strange city. Pedestrians walk along the elevated wooden sidewalks and across the many arched bridges that connect the old buildings to one another. Every now and then you see a plaza where people are getting their morning coffee or bagels from pushcarts.

"Here you are," says the captain as he pulls up to a fancy looking dock with an awning and a uniformed steward to help guests disembark. "Have fun in the high rent district."

The lobby of Preston Billings' building is sleek, modern, and old-fashioned at the same time. Marble is everywhere, and you see gilt accents all over the place. You have never been in a lobby as fancy as this.

"You may go right up," says the beautiful but cold receptionist. "Here is the key to the elevator. Just wave it in front of door number twelve. Mr. Billings did not inform me that you had guests, but I instant-messaged him and he said that your friends could come up as well. Have a nice day."

Turn to page 113.

Back to School

"Sorry, we don't have the money, and besides, we can't just abandon Peter's car; it has all of our stuff in it," you tell Lucas Foren. "Thanks for the offer though."

"Listen kids, I don't want you to get the impression that I am pressuring you, but there is strange stuff going down here. I don't care if you don't want to join me, but forget about the car. You can always try the human train system. It's slow, but you could probably make it to New York within a few days," he says, standing up from his table and putting his tablet away. "Here's my card with my landline number. Just give me a call if you run into trouble with the Gatekeepers."

"Thanks," says Peter, also standing up. "But we'll be fine."

"I hope so. Good luck," says Foren as he leaves the café. As you watch him go you wonder if you made the right choice.

"He was probably just a weirdo," says Dresdale, but she doesn't sound as confident as she normally does. "What kind of name is that anyway? It sounds like something from a play or something."

"Come on, let's get going. We need to find a place to stay tonight before we go to our hearing tomorrow."

You leave the café after asking about the nearest, cheapest hotel. "You're not runaways are you?" asks the café waitress, but when you assure that you are not, she tells you about a bed and breakfast run by a friend of hers. "Not many people stay overnight in strange towns these days," she says, pointing the way. "Watch out for the Gatekeepers!"

"I felt bad about lying to her," you say as you walk through a quiet residential neighborhood. All the houses are neat and tidy, with nice lawns. "'Cause we are sort of runaways."

"But we're trying to find your parents, not get away from them!" says Dresdale. "Besides, if old Schliemann Scary-Pants hadn't gotten us kicked out of Alstone, we'd still be there."

"I guess you're right, but it still feels like we are doing something wrong somehow."

"I know how you feel," says Peter. "But we haven't done anything wrong. Something wrong has been done to us."

After walking for about twenty minutes, you arrive at the B&B. The owner tries to turn you away since the three of you are minors, but you can tell business has been slow, so after agreeing to pay for three separate rooms, she agrees to let you stay. "Don't use all of the hot water, and don't tell the Gatekeepers that I let you stay here!"

"Man, people seem really freaked out about the Gatekeepers around here," says Peter, sitting on the bed in your room. Dresdale is in the one chair, and you are perched on the old desk that is wedged into the tiny space. "What do you think is going on?"

"I don't know," replies Dresdale, after thinking for a bit. "But I don't like it. Maybe it has something to do with the insurgency?"

"Must be," you agree. "Although I have never heard of anything happening this far south. Most of the activity has always been in the northeast, near the old Canadian border where the Quebec separatists come from."

"My mom was talking about how bad things have been getting for a lot of people when I went home after Carlsbad," says Dresdale. "She said that even people who used to support the government were getting tired of all the new restrictions and rules. Of course, none of that ever gets reported in the mainstream media, but those were the rumors that she was hearing. Apparently they captured a cell of insurgents who were going to attack the main Gatekeeper office in Chicago. That's a long way from Quebec, so clearly the insurgency is spreading beyond the northeast."

"Hey, guys," interrupts Peter. "I know I slept some in the back, but I am so tired after yesterday and today that I have to hit the hay. Besides, I just want to get to the hearing and get my car back."

"Yeah, I'm beat too," agrees Dresdale, stifling a yawn. "See you two in the morning."

After your friends leave, you try and fall asleep, but your mind is racing so fast that you feel as if you are going to spin off the bed. You take a hot shower, and that helps, but mindful of the owner's warning about the hot water, you hop out before you really want to.

"Oh Mom, Dad, I miss you," you say out loud into the darkness. You feel like a little kid. Helpless and alone. You don't know what you would do if you did not have Peter and Dresdale with you. By the time morning light shows in your window, you have slept a bit, but you are worn out and tired, not refreshed.

"Rise and shine, sleepyhead," says Peter with a grin from your door. Once again, he looks as though he has been staying in a spa, while you feel like you have been sleeping by the side of the road.

"I'm awake," you say.

"Are you all right?" he says, the grin disappearing.

"Not really," you reply, trying to keep the tears from your eyes and your voice.

"Listen, when my parents died, I felt like I was dying too. But I didn't. I still miss them more than anything in the world, and that will never go away, but we don't know what happened to your parents. They might be fine and we'll catch up with them soon."

"They might be dead, too," you say, giving voice to your deepest fear. "Or worse. Tortured or trapped somewhere."

"You can't think like that," says Peter, taking your hand in his. It is warm and dry. "We need to think positively to get through this. It is the only way. Come on, let's go get my car back!"

The walk to the hearing court takes a long time, but at least you have a full belly to keep you moving. The B&B owner made the three of you a great blueberry pancake breakfast, but she would not give you a ride to the courthouse. "Sorry kids, things are mixed up right now, and I don't want to get caught up in it. Remember, don't tell them that I let you stay here!"

"Please report to the second floor," says the bored clerk as you show your receipt from Peter's car impounding. As you enter the room where the hearing is set, you get a sense of foreboding that makes you want to turn around and leave without going through the process, but it is Peter's car, not yours, so you go ahead.

"Case Number 1089. What is your reason for driving without adult supervision?" says the Gatekeeper hearing judge. He is middle-aged, overweight, bald, and he does not look up from the pile of papers on his desk. There are no chairs to sit in, so the three of you stand.

"We were going to meet my parents in New York," you say, feeling uneasy about the lie, and wondering if you would actually meet your parents again.

"Unfortunately, that is not a valid reason. The Transportation Doctrine is very clear about that. Your papers require you to have adult supervision. Your vehicle is forfeit as a penalty." The hearing judge says this all very quickly and with almost no inflection in his voice.

"You can't do that!" shouts Peter. "We haven't done anything wrong!"

"Come on, don't make him mad," hisses Dresdale to Peter. You are about to grab Peter by the arm and get him out of there when the door opens and the clerk from the front comes running into the room. He hands the hearing judge a slip of paper, points at the three of you, and then runs back out of the room.

"I have just been informed that the three of you are wanted back at your school."

"What!?" you exclaim. Fingers of apprehension scroll down your back. "What do they want? We were expelled."

The fat, unpleasant official glances at his computer screen, squints, and smiles in an unfriendly way. "Anybody's guess. Don't look a gift horse in the mouth, kid."

You hate him, and search the room for an exit. But it's futile. At that moment, three Gatekeepers in their stupid dark blue uniforms with red collar tabs burst in, weapons drawn.

The smallest and meanest looking of them speaks; his voice is high, thin, and whiny.

"Don't be frightened. This is good news. Better than you deserve," he says, smirking. "Your school wants you back. All is forgiven!"

"Don't jerk us around," Dres says, a hard note in her voice.

"Be nice. If it were up to me, you three would go on a nice long voyage to nowhere for the rest of time, but I'm here to tell you that an amnesty has been granted—an amnesty from the very top. Don't blow it."

Peter makes a move but is blocked by one of the Gatekeepers.

"Boy, you kids are nothing but trouble. Sometimes the gift horse bites back," he adds with a sadistic smile. "Stun him."

ZAP!!!

A sharp, a tongue of lightning leaps from a taser and Peter crumples to the ground. He flops and moans.

"OK, out of here. Let's go," one of the Gatekeepers says, waving the taser.

Dresdale looks white as a sheet. You imagine that you don't look much better. Outside the dismal office building rests a weird looking contraption, part rocket and part hovercraft. Its colors are faded, but you can make out the insignia of a long-gone nation that led the way in air transport.

"All aboard," the smarmy Gatekeeper says. The other two Gatekeepers load Peter onboard as though he were a sack of potatoes. He moans weakly. You fear for his life, but when you move to check him, you are brushed back with a smack to the face. "Don't touch," the captain snarls.

It takes an amazingly short time to get to the playing fields of good old Alstone where the craft makes a rough landing.

"All out, no fooling around. My job ends here," the smarmy one says.

Dres and you help Peter, who is now coming around, off the craft; it rumbles like an old furnace and then lifts off. The captain waves from a porthole, a smile of wicked pleasure on his face. You three are alone on the empty playing fields, but not for long. Mr. Cummings, the headmaster, and two teachers run forward; they are accompanied by two Gatekeepers. This doesn't look good, you think.

"Welcome back," Cummings says with a half smile on his now haggard face. "I got you a second chance, a hard thing to do with this current environment."

"Thanks, but why? And where are my parents and Mr. Rimy?" you ask.

"All will be explained, but I have to caution you. Any attempt by you to leave Alstone again and Dresdale will be imprisoned on Orcas Island in the maximum-security cell block there until you return."

The two officials grab Dresdale and handcuff her.

"Please come with us, Miss," they say without emotion.

You look at Mr. Cummings. "It's not my idea. I've done all I can," he says.

Days later, with Dresdale guarded around the clock, you and Peter are back in class, examples of what happens to people who defy the government. People pretend you don't even exist. To borrow a phrase from your dad, you have been sent to Coventry.

Your parents are still missing. Cummings and the other teachers make noise about tracking them down, but it's just that: noise.

They lied about that to get you to come with them. Now you are caught. Gatekeepers patrol the grounds of the school. Everyone is afraid.

Several days later, an email appears from your mother's dead-letter email account. There is no sender's address. It says:

Nessum doro. Nunc dimitus. Illuminati. Fratres Gaudiosi.

It's sloppy Latin, but the word Illuminati sparkles and projects the words: Wait. Hope. Overcome.

When you show it to Dresdale on your daily fifteen-minute visit, she exclaims, "This is part of a prophecy."

"What does it mean?" you ask. "And what is the prophecy?"

"It means that the future is with the Illuminated Ones. Help will come, but not from Earthlings."

Dresdale is getting thinner. You wonder how long you must wait…

The End

The Radiant Ones

"You go on ahead, then. I'll just check it out, Peter."

You head off across the field in the direction of the flash. It is due west of you; it might have been a reflection from the rising sun.

You cross the field. The smell of the wheat is heavy and sweet. A low hill blocks your view. You climb it and look toward where you saw the flash.

"Oh, my god!" you exclaim as you see a small settlement that has been completely destroyed. Smoldering ruins mark its outline. Everything has been burnt. Some buildings are completely gone, but others are still standing. Strangely, the trees and telephone poles are free of any fire damage. You move forward to find out more.

Was it a small town? It consists of just a few buildings, but they are separate and not close together. You don't understand how the fire traveled from place to place. There aren't any cars or people around and that makes you nervous. You walk up to

a white farmhouse that is only partially destroyed and look in. Everything is covered in gray dust and ash, and you see black, cut-out shapes of people on the walls of the kitchen. It's as if they had been burnt suddenly and totally.

There are more black silhouettes of people on the outsides of their houses. These outlines are of people cowering in fear, with their arms raised up protectively, not of people leaning casually against a wall or playing. They remind you of something and then you remember. It looks like the permanent shadows left behind by a nuclear blast. You saw pictures of those in a textbook about Hiroshima and Nagasaki in Japan after the old United States bombed them.

"What are you doing here?" The voice is angry and low. You

turn around and see a man with a shotgun pointed straight at your heart.

"Nuh, nothing!" you say, moving backwards and bumping up against the wall of the burnt farmhouse. You raise your hands half way to show they're empty.

"Who are you?" he asks. The question would sound normal, except for the fact that the gun is still pointed at your chest.

"I was on that hill! I came over after I saw a bright flash!"

The man lowers the gun a bit. His face is dirty and tired-looking. "You shouldn't be here. They might come back. Keep your hands where I can see them!"

"Who might come back? The farmers?"

"None of them will be making it back here," the man says with a despairing laugh. "This is a bad place to be. You should leave."

"What happened here?" you ask, careful to keep your hands in plain view.

"I don't know. I don't know," says the man, and you think that he might cry, as his face twists and his voice gets thick. "A week ago, this was a small town, just like any other. Now everyone is gone. Killed, I think. All that is left are these shadows on the walls. My sister and her whole family used to live here."

"I'm sorry," you say. "Did anyone survive?"

"Only Bobby Fields. He's five. He said he was hiding in the tall grass to play a trick on his sister. It was early evening, when the shadows are long. Everything went bright, and he said he saw shining people walking out of the fire. They went from house to house. Looking for something. Each time they went to a house, these shining people would flare up and the people would fry and the house would catch on fire. That poor little kid."

"Where is he now?" you ask.

"Oh, the government people came and took him to the hospital. I stayed away from them. I know better than to mess with them. They only left a day ago, but I think they will be back. Something horrible happened here, but I don't think they knew what any better than I do."

The man stops talking and eyes you carefully.

"Are you a runaway? It doesn't matter. You should get out of here. Now."

"Why?" you ask.

He pauses.

"Because your parents want you to." His eyes flash a brilliant blue; they look like laser beams. Suddenly they dim and go blank.

"My parents? What about my parents! Who are you?" you cry. You step toward the man, forgetting the gun. He seems to dematerialize into a cord of shining silver.

"You are young. You understand little. Your parents did not do the right job with you." You yell, "Tell me!! Tell me what to do."

It is as though his spirit has taken over.

"Your parents belong to the FFA! Forget them. They are beyond hope."

"NO! NO! I don't believe you." There is no time for tears. You summon your own formidable energy, grasp the spinning silver cable, and squeeze as hard as you can. "What is the FFA and where are they?!"

The spinning stops and the old man emerges just as he was before.

"The FFA stands for the Freedom Forever Alliance. Insurgents in plain language."

"How do you know?"

"Because I belong to the FFA. I was their guide into the group. Everyone needs a guide to vouch for them. I was your father's professor and thesis advisor in college—his best friend. I introduced him to the FFA."

You are stunned. How do such coincidences happen? What is the nature of these mysteries? What can you do?

"But, but…he never mentioned you. What is your name? What did you teach?"

"My name is secret. The FAA is secret. I taught semiotics."

"Semiotics? What in the world is that?" you stammer.

"It is the study of signs and symbols. They are all around us and affect our lives."

"I don't understand. But my dad, my mom?"

"I can't say any more. My job is over now, at least for the time being. I drove the Radiant Ones from this cursed spot; I and my three colleagues. There they are, mere shadows on a wall." He points to the silhouettes on the wall of the burnt building.

"My parents?"

"They know too much for their own good. Too much about the Inner Earth, a realm of both light and darkness where both good and evil joust with each other for control."

"What are you talking about?" Your head is spinning. Maybe he is just a crazy. Maybe he is here to lead you astray. Or maybe this is just a bad dream?

But then how did he know who you were? How did he know about your parents?

"The Inner Earth is like a Mobious strip, once on it, you never get off...unless you break the strip."

"What are you talking about? Inner Earth is just out of the comic books of years ago. It's a fable, a kid's story."

"If that is what you think, then leave! You'll never find your parents—little good it will do anyway if you do." He seems to be shrinking, becoming less and less human, more concept than reality. "There are many ways into the Inner Earth. Carlsbad Caverns is only one way. And it is a dangerous way. The Radiant Ones control one of the secret entrance gates. They kill all who know or try to find the path. They followed me and my colleagues here to this simple town and destroyed it in an orgy of hate.

"My parents. How long? Why? Where now?" you can barely speak.

"Seek them in the Inner Earth. But Carlsbad is clogged now. It has drawn too much attention to itself. Big Sur is the place now. Few know of that entrance." He gives a sudden pause.

"That is all I can tell you. I must go."

He fades to nothing, like so much wood smoke in open air.

You turn around and run as fast as you can back to Dresdale and Peter.

Continue on your quest on page 52 of The Golden Path Volume II: Burned By The Inner Sun

Good luck.

Ungava Bay

You pay the water taxi and hurry to Lucas Foren's body shop.

"The three musketeers are back," he jokes when you round the corner. "How did it go?"

"We need your help, Lucas. Here's your money. All of it!" you say as you push eight more hundreds into Lucas' grease-covered palm. "Can you take us to Ungava Bay?"

"Quebec?" Lucas says, looking down at the money in his hand. He stuffs it into his pocket and turns to you. "Right in the middle of the FFA country. Things are hot up there. What happened to you all?"

You, Dresdale, and Peter are shaking. You have never seen someone die before, let alone seen someone murdered right in front of your eyes. Someone you knew.

"Let's just say that something bad happened in New York. We'll tell you more later. That is if you can take us to Ungava. Mr. Billings told me that was where I could pick up my parents' trail. He said not to trust the public transport system.

The Gatekeepers will be all over us. He also gave me more money. We can pay you!"

"Calm down," Lucas says, clearly playing for time. "Hold on a minute. I have way too much work to do here. Besides, I'm not a taxi service."

"You said before that you had some time off," Dresdale blurts. "Please, we need your help. They murdered him right in front of us!"

"Murdered who? What are you talking about?"

"They threw him out of his window. We had just been with him. He hit the stone steps. His name was Preston Billings," Peter says. "Please, help us!"

Lucas whistles and looks at each of you in turn. "Man, you guys are like a sack full of kittens. I don't know whether to throw you in the river or take you home and feed you!"

"Thank you, Lucas," Dresdale says, putting her hand on his forearm.

"I didn't say I'd do it!" Foren protests, but he doesn't pull away.

"I think they're following us," you say. "I don't know how, but I think they are. They were probably going up in the elevator while we were coming down." You shiver at the thought. You have never been afraid of heights, but the thought of being thrown out of the fortieth floor of a building makes you cringe.

"Four thousand," says Lucas. "And that is the cheapest I can do."

You take out the envelope and remove several hundred dollar bills and hand the rest to Foren. "Here you go."

"Okay. Okay. We'll take the electrical repair van. These babies are always needed due to the FFA taking power lines down all the time. We'll be able to go anywhere. Also, they can charge up by linking into the power grid via any live line. Come on. I'll get the keys."

Before noon, you have been to the supermarket, a sporting goods store, and a bookstore. "Feed your mind," says Lucas as you look at a book about the Arctic. "But do it once we are on the road." He pays for everything: the jackets, the food, the boots, and all the other gear. By the time you are done with your whirlwind shopping spree, you doubt that Lucas will be making much money on this trip.

"What are the zip ties for?" Peter asks, holding up a plastic tube with dozens of multi-color, multi-length zip ties.

"You can do amazing things with zip ties," Foren explains once you are on the highway. "Make water pouches, clamp hoses, tie off bleeding wounds."

"Have you ever tied off a wound with a zip tie?" Peter asks from the middle row seat. Even with all of the electrical equipment and your expedition supplies, the van is still spacious and comfortable. For the first time you feel like you are on an adventure, and then you remember Mr. Billings, then Tito, and then your parents.

"Not personally, but I've seen it done. A guy in the first garage that I worked in almost cut his hand off. Big Tony had him wrapped up and tied off in no time flat. Anyway, I don't mean to scare you, but we are heading into a civil war zone. The gov press won't call it that, but that's what is going on up there."

"What is going on up there? I mean specifically?" you ask,

not really knowing the latest situation of the FFA's insurgency.

"No one knows for sure. They keep a news blackout for the most part. Except when they have something good to report. It's been very rare lately. So, by the absence, we conclude that things must be going well for the FFA."

"You're not a typical mechanic are you?" Dresdale asks, looking up from her book. She still hasn't been able to get in touch with either of her parents. You know that she is worried.

"Define typical," replies Lucas with a touch of ire. "All mechanics are problem solvers. It is part of the job. Hold on a second. We have a big Gatekeeper operation up ahead."

You see a long line of cars in front of you, but Foren pulls onto the shoulder of the road and turns on his emergency lights. The yellow-orange flashes definitely give the van an official look, or so it seems to you.

"We're heading up north to help with the power outages," Lucas says easily to the Gatekeeper as he casually cuts in front of a sedan with a family and all of their luggage. You can't tell whether they are going on vacation or fleeing for their lives. "We need to get there as soon as possible."

The Gatekeeper looks at Lucas Foren without smiling. All you can see of his face is his close-shaven chin; his eyes and nose are hidden behind a visor and a helmet. Gatekeepers have always made you uneasy. "This unit is showing in the SecureNet that it's in for repairs. Please advise."

"Of course it is," Lucas says reasonably. "We just had it fixed this morning. We need to get back to check it in as being functional."

"Very good. You are cleared for travel. Be warned, there has been substantial rebel activity north of here recently. We've lost a couple of patrols outside of Manchester New Hampshire. You know how those 'live free or die' nuts are. Be careful."

"Will do. How are the road conditions?"

"Variable. They vary from bad to worse, but it won't be too bad this time of year. Sleet season won't start until late December."

"Thanks for the info!" Lucas says easily as he rolls up the window and drives the van forward.

You curl up in the back, next to the reserve jerry cans of synth-fuel. They slosh and make a liquid sound each time you go over a bump. Lucas thought that there was no sense risking being stranded in case the grid went down. You agree, but you are not sure that you would have thought of bringing the extra fuel.

Sleep creeps up and you go from dozing to a dream where Schliemann is giving you your trigonometry test. Midway through, he rips off his mask of a face and it is your father. You gasp awake. Peter and Dresdale are sprawled out on the seats in front of you. Lucas is driving and the lights from the dashboard give him a spectral look. He is staring intently at the road, as there is a light rain falling.

"Where are we?" you ask as you move into the front seat and buckle in.

"Just south of the old Canadian border. We made good time through Massachusetts. My guess is that things will start to get interesting near Old Montreal. The last time the FFA poked its head above ground, they had street fighting until they used knockout gas on the whole city. Over five thousand people never woke up from that. Little kids and old people mostly. It did stop the fighting pretty quickly though. You got to give them that," Lucas says with deep bitterness and begrudging admiration. You wonder where those feelings came from.

"Did you lose someone from there?"

"Not me personally. Well, sort of. It's hard to explain. A good friend of mine, well, her mom and niece both died when they used the gas. I never knew them. I met her a long time after that happened. Still."

"No problems near Manchester?" You ask, looking for a safer topic.

"Quiet as a dead baby," Lucas says, kind of killing the conversation for a little while. You watch the leaves and the water on the old roads. You don't see many cars or other vehicles out and about. It all seems a bit spooky and unreal. You see a patch of darker night further off in the distance. The rain is coming down harder now, and you don't know for sure what it is, but it is dark, dark, and close.

You freeze. Time stands still as one word enters your brain: *Moose.* You have never seen one, but you know what it is. Right in front of you. Standing in the middle of the road. Right in front of you! You don't think Lucas has seen it. Time starts again. You have a heartbeat to decide what to do.

If you yell a warning and brace for impact, turn to page 73.

If you grab the wheel and try and move the electrical van out of the way, turn to page 130.

Wyrms

We can't leave Rimy," you shout "Dresdale, Peter, the three of us can get him and meet Durno!"

"This is madness. I said they released the Wyrm Hounds!" says Durno from the doorway. "Stay and die, or follow me."

"Are you sure about this?" asks Peter. "Durno sounded pretty convinced that this was a bad idea. What are Wyrm Hounds anyway?"

"I think the Wyrm probably refers to ancient myths about dragons, but the hounds part means that they probably aren't dragons," Dresdale explains quickly. "Maybe it means they use them to hunt dragons?"

"That sounds like something I don't want to meet," you say while running across the room. "But we have no choice!"

Dresdale and Peter follow you closely as you head down the corridors of the rebel encampment. You realize that it is a lot bigger than you thought, and you have no idea where the council room is. None of the Lemurians talk to you. Most seem to be trying to get out of the base.

Clanging, banging and screaming fills the air. A smart marching line of Lemurians holding gunlike tubes go past the three of you. Not knowing what else to do, you follow them.

You enter a huge hanger carved out of the rock, where the Lemurians are fighting a fierce battle with swarms of black-clad figures. You assume they must be the attacking Agarthans. Smoke and dust obscure your sight, but you see many dead Lemurians scattered among the broken hulks of huge machines. There are a few Agarthans as well, but not many. The three of you take cover behind one of the piles of broken machinery.

"This is worse than a movie," yells Peter in your ear. "I think we should find Durno. We have no idea where Rimy is!"

"You're right," you yell back, but as you are about to continue, a gut-shuddering cry echoes through the hanger. You peek above the edge of your cover and immediately let out a low cry of surprise. "Run!"

Feeling stuck, you watch as the Wyrm Hound comes bounding into the hanger, looking for prey. Tall and long, it has four powerful legs that end in paws with rough-looking sharp claws. Adorned in a dull brownish-red pelt, you can't take your gaze off of its two darting heads.

One of the heads is small and blade-shaped, on the end of a long neck, making it look almost like an elephant's trunk. Two beady eyes stare out from little pits over its mouth. When it snaps its mouth open, you see long teeth, but the other head is worse.

Underneath the long trunklike neck is a more normal-looking head and neck, but only by comparison. The lower head has two huge eyes and a prominent nose. Two large tusks jut from its jaw, and rows of other sharp teeth gnash and grind as the hound searches for prey. You feel a tap on your shoulder, and you realize you have just been standing there without moving.

"I'm coming, Peter," you whisper as you turn around.

It was not Peter tapping you on the shoulder, though. The last thing you see is a head full of teeth shooting at you like a predator eel from its cave.

The End

Continued from page 87

After the elevator ride, you pass through another level of receptionists. These ones have slightly more genuine smiles and they wave you right in to Preston Billings' office.

"Welcome! I'm so glad you made it," he says, coming around his massive glass and gold desk. "You look just like your parents. I could have spotted you a mile off."

He is shorter than you had imagined him, with thinning blond hair and a squinty look as though he spent too much time staring at a computer screen. His smile is broad, though, and he does look glad to see you. "Who are you friends?"

"This is Peter Kim and Dresdale Hamilton. We were all kicked out of Alstone together," you say as means of introduction. Seeing him hesitate, you add. "You can talk openly in front of them. I trust my friends completely and so do my mom and dad. You said on the phone that you had information about my parents. And that you could only tell me in person."

"Yes. Sad but true," says Billings. "This world is becoming crazier by the minute. I just hope that we can talk safely here. If we can't I'm done for anyway, so what the heck!"

"Do you know where my parents are?" you ask, desperation making your voice sound funny in your ears. "I'm really worried about them, Mr. Billings."

"Dianna and Donald were supposed to meet me two days ago for dinner, but they never showed up. They had plans to go to Ungava Bay with Alphonse Rimy. I believe you know, him, correct?"

"Rimy was going to meet your parents?" Peter asks.

"Isn't Ungava Bay in the middle of the FFA's insurgency?" interrupts Dresdale. "Why were they going there?"

"Ungava is in what was once northern Quebec," Mr. Billings answers as you all talk at once. "And yes, they were going there to meet Alphonse Rimy about some sort of expedition into the Arctic around the North Pole. I don't know all of the details. They needed a lot of money to fund the expedition. Which is why we were meeting. They had to sign the documents in person, due to the large sum of money."

"How much money?" you ask. "We've never been rich."

Preston Billings laughs. "That may have been the case once," he says, "but no longer. You are rich. Perhaps not super-rich, but very rich indeed. Your parents were going to transfer $42 million to the project. They would have had quite a bit left after that. I think that if you want to find your parents, you need to go to Ungava Bay. If there is any way that they haven't been taken, then they would go there. If they have been taken, you won't be able to find them."

"But why Ungava? I still don't get it. Their archeological specialty was the southwest, places like Carlsbad. Why would they go north into ice country?" you ask. You don't want to think about the possibility that your parents have been taken, even though part of you feels that it is the most real of all the possibilities. "Why go into the middle of the insurgency?"

"I don't mean to be rude," says Billings quietly, glancing at Dresdale and Peter, "but are you absolutely sure you can trust your friends? This isn't some child's game your parents are caught up in."

"I trust Dres and Peter with my life," you say. You mean it but it still sounds strange. You feel a bit like an actor in a play.

"Okay then," he begins before pausing and taking a deep breath. "Your parents have been working with the FFA to help overthrow our current crop of dictators. I have been helping them. At first, I didn't know anything about what they were doing. I thought I was helping to manage their money for retirement. I'm no radical, believe me. However, like many working against the current government, I felt compelled by the steady erosion of personal and professional rights to do something. Helping your parents became the way for me to do my part."

"Wait a second," you interject. "My parents are members of the insurgency?"

Billings just looks at you with one of those world-weary smiles that adults use when they think you are just "too young to understand."

"Listen, the insurgency has caught up all sorts of people who would not be in it unless the situation was getting desperate. Like I said, I personally have never been very political; all I was interested in was business and finance. However, over the last few years, things have gotten so bad that even people like me have joined the process. I think you would be surprised just how many citizens are working against the totalitarianism of the current government and our puppet

President." Billings sighs. "Or who are working as spies and informers for that government," he finishes darkly. "Your parents were clear that if anything happened to them, I was supposed to help you in any way I can, and to get you to meet up with Rimy in Ungava Bay if possible."

As he says this, he goes to his desk and rummages around for a moment before pulling out a plain white envelope. He hands it to you. It is thick.

"Take this," he says. "Sorry I don't have more on hand, but I don't normally keep much cash around. You three should find a hotel here in the city for tonight. I'll get in touch with my people and arrange a secure transport for you to the Ungava Bay area. That is, if you want me to, but it is what your parents asked me to do. I highly recommend you take their advice. Things might be dangerous for you if you don't."

"That isn't a threat, is it?" asks Peter, standing straight and trying to look tough.

"Oh god, no!" says Billings. "Look, I'm not very good at this stuff. I'm just trying to warn you and let you know how serious this whole situation is. Will you go to Ungava Bay? I'll arrange the transportation and I'll be able to give you more money tomorrow. Lord knows your parents would want me to!"

"I guess we'll go then," you say. "Thanks."

Your head has been spinning for the last couple of days. The latest news doesn't seem to be affecting you as much as you would expect. Spies! Your parents are spies working for the FFA? It seems unbelievable to you, but would Preston

Billings make all this up? Heading to Ungava Bay to meet Rimy sounds like a reasonable thing to do in an unreasonable situation.

"Good," your parents' financial advisor says. "I'm glad." He is smiling and sweating, even in the cool air of his air-conditioned office. You feel like shivering. "I'll have everything taken care of. Come by tomorrow at nine and we'll get you on your way. Right now I have an important meeting, so why don't the three of you see the sights in the city?"

"Thanks, Mr. Billings," you say, shaking his sweaty hand. He squeezes you on the shoulder and looks into your eyes.

"I will do the best I can for you. That is the least I can do for your parents."

"Do you think he always sweats that much?" Peter asks in the elevator. "It was freezing in there!"

"How much money did he give you?"

"I don't know, Dres, but it feels like a lot," you say, looking into the envelope. It's stuffed with hundred dollar notes. "Three grand, at least. Maybe four."

"Wow!" says Peter. "Can we eat breakfast at the Plaza? 'Cause I am starving!"

"You are a glutton," Dresdale says disapprovingly, "but I'm hungry too."

You leave Preston Billings' office building and hire another water taxi.

"Where to?" the captain asks, pushing away from the dock to let another boat come in.

A loud crash of breaking glass stops you from speaking.

You look up to see a large black chair and broken glass come showering down from Preston Billings' building.

"What the—" Dresdale shouts, but before she can finish her sentence, another object drops from the sky. This one, however, has arms, legs, and a head, all of which are jerking and writhing. Screams shatter the air as you watch the body fall. It hits the stone steps of the building and bounces before lying still. Blood spatters on impact, turning the doorman's blue suit a bright red.

"Oh God! It's Mr. Billings," Peter whispers in your ear. "We need to get out of here, now!" The shock overwhelms you. You just stare at the lifeless pile that was a person mere moments before.

"Is he dead?" Dresdale's face is pale, but her voice is calm.

"There isn't anything we can do for him," you say. "He fell from the fortieth floor. Peter is right. We need to get out of here. Now!"

"Why would he jump out of the window?" Dresdale asks. "He seemed nervous, but not like he was suicidal or anything."

"I don't think he jumped," you answer, with your heart beating fast in your chest "I think he was pushed. Captain! Can…Can you take us to Brooklyn?"

"Yeah," says the taxi captain. "I don't think I want to be here any longer, either. Bad things have been happening too often lately."

The captain cranks the steering wheel and pushes the throttle all the way forward. The boat jumps forward and you stumble from the acceleration. As the dock of the building recedes, you can see that a small crowd of people surrounds Preston Billings' dead body. You feel sick.

"What the hell is going on?" Peter asks. "What should we do? Do you think we should listen to Billings and go to Ungava Bay? These people are playing for keeps. We're next, I'll bet."

Waves from the speeding taxi hit the docks and sides of buildings. Other boaters wave at the taxi captain angrily as his wake hits them. He ignores them.

"Let's pay Lucas Foren and then make a plan," you say. "Maybe he can take us to Ungava Bay? It's probably too dangerous traveling on our own right now. We need help. Or someplace safe to lie low for a while."

"I have an aunt who lives in Southport, Connecticut," Dresdale says. She is shaking and her lips are thin and colorless. It is not from cold, as the morning sun is now shining brightly down on you as you cross the East Hudson Delta toward Brooklyn. "She could put us up for a couple of nights for sure, and maybe we could figure out how to get to Ungava Bay with her help?"

"I wouldn't mind sleeping in a bed for a change," Peter says, "but I'll do whatever you think is best for finding your parents." He looks at you intently.

"Do you trust your aunt?" you ask Dresdale. "How well do you know her? And when was the last time that you saw her?"

"Of course I trust her! Otherwise I wouldn't mention her. She doesn't have any kids of her own. Her husband, my uncle Frank, passed away a couple of years ago. She loves having visitors. She's great," Dresdale says defensively, as if you are attacking her family.

"Sorry" you say. "But after what we saw today, I we can't afford to take any chances. I'm sure Mr. Billings death has something to do with our visit. Or that's my fear."

"So what do you want to do?" asks Peter. "We're almost to Brooklyn."

If you decide to talk to Lucas Foren and see if you can convince him to take you to Ungava Bay, turn to page 104.

If you decide to lie low for awhile and go to Dresdale's aunt's house in Connecticut, go on to the next page.

The Ninth Ring

You head to the garage in Brooklyn and pay Lucas Foren the money you owe him, but he will only take a thousand total. "Don't worry about the rest," he says, tucking the fresh bills inside his jacket pocket. At first his price seemed like a rip-off, but now you feel like you got a good deal.

"Where to now?" he asks, eyeing the three of you. It's as if he can sense something bad has happened. "You all okay?"

"We're fine. We thought we'd go stay with family friends, in Connecticut," Dresdale chimes in.

"Just make sure you can trust 'em," Lucas replies after a long pause. "Best way to Connecticut is the commuter train. The station is five blocks south of here," he adds. pointing down the street from the dark cave of his garage. "Give me a call if you need help, but don't write my number down, just memorize it. 89-90-81-76," he rattles off quickly. "Good luck! I think that you are going to need it."

You are still in shock, but you nod and keep moving. You repeat the phone number silently a few times to make sure you have it.

"Thanks, Lucas. We wouldn't have made it here without you. Are you sure you won't take your full price?"

"Don't worry, kid. What kind of a friend would I be if I charged you two hundred bucks for a couple of hours? Just keep your heads up. Things are dangerous these days, as I think you know." He stands signaling it's time to leave. "I got to go. Tony and Matt can't tie their shoes without my help, and they need me on the floor."

You walk to the station. Dresdale calls her aunt from a local pay phone there. She has to put in her identity badge to activate the phone, and you worry about that, but there is nothing you can do. Hopefully no one is looking for her.

The phone rings nine times before someone picks up. You had given up hope, but loyal Dresdale stayed on. She quickly asks her aunt if you can stay with her.

"Thanks, Aunt Carrie! I knew I could count on you! We'll catch the 12:35." She hangs up the phone and smiles at the two of you. "She said she'd come to the station there to pick us up."

"C'mon, we'll only catch it if we hustle," you say. The train station is almost empty at midday. You look to see if someone is watching you. All you know about spying is from books or movies. Everything looks normal.

"Three tickets to Southport," says Dresdale to the ticket woman.

"Round trip or one way?" the clerk asks.

"One way, thanks."

The train is almost forty minutes late, but once you are moving you relax. Then you remember Preston Billings hitting the stone steps with a sick thud. You don't feel relaxed anymore. When you think of Tito and your parents, a wave of nausea hits. Peter rests with his head back and eyes closed, while Dresdale looks out the window as the scenery slowly changes from city to suburb.

"Remember, Dres, we are just on a class trip and we ran into a booking problem at the hotel," you remind your friend.

"I don't think that will work," she says, looking at you with her pale blue eyes, all seriousness. "I'll have to call my parents again, and I already told them that we were kicked out of school and that I was staying with you. We have to tell her the truth."

"Maybe," you say, "but not the whole truth, okay? You saw what happened to Preston Billings. Whoever is after us is playing for keeps. I don't want your aunt getting mixed up in this in a bad way."

"Yes, I did see what happened to him," she says, looking down. A tear hits her folded-up hands and slides down to the seats. You pass the rest of the trip in silence, each with your own thoughts.

"Wake up," you say, nudging Peter awake. "We're here."

"Dresdale! Over here!" yells a woman waving in the parking lot of the train station. She is neatly dressed in a blue cardigan and a long skirt. Her hair looks long, but it is hard to tell, as it is pulled up into a tight bun. She has on large, fancy-looking sunglasses and she smiles at the three of you brightly.

"Aunt Carrie! Thanks for coming to get us! These are my friends," she says, waving vaguely at you and Peter. You wish that you had had time to clean up some more, but the two of you stand up straight and try to look presentable.

"Oh, Dresdale, look how you have grown! You're a young woman now! The last time I saw you were still just a little girl. Come on kids, hop in. My house is just around the corner."

Aunt Carrie's small white convertible convinces you that she must be rich. The car has wood paneling, and everything gleams in an expensive way. This impression of wealth is confirmed when you pull up a long driveway to a large house.

"I'll have Charles take your things, you can freshen up, and then we can have dinner and you can catch me up on what you've been up to!"

Each of you is taken to your own room with its own bathroom and sitting area. Your window overlooks a wide green lawn with a row of trees against a high wall. Even though it is fall, and the trees are ablaze with yellows, reds and oranges mixed with the occasional green, there are no leaves on the grass. Someone must stay very busy making sure of that.

You try to relax by taking a bath and doing some stretching, but nothing seems to work. When you think back to this morning, your breath starts to come fast out of your mouth and you feel like you are about to faint.

"Hey, can I come in?" Peter asks as he knocks on your door.

"Sure," you answer, glad to have him there. "What's up? We should be getting ready for dinner, it's almost six o'clock."

"Why are we here?" he asks, sitting down on the pale chintz chair in the corner of the big room. "I don't mean to tell you what to do, but I was thinking about it some more, and if we are going to find your parents, I'm not sure being in Southport, Connecticut is doing anything."

Your belly tightens with the knowledge that Peter is right. "I don't know, but after what has happened today, and over the last couple of days, I felt that we needed time to rest up in a safe place."

"Yeah, maybe. That's what I thought before, but something doesn't feel right. I think that we should get out of here as soon as we can."

"You're probably right, but what do we tell Dresdale? Sorry that you got your aunt to take us in, but we're going to head off into the dark without Gatekeeper papers. Oh and can you put dinner in a bag for us?"

"Well, we couldn't say that, but I still don't like this place. Maybe it is just that I have never been in a house this fancy before. I mean, I guess you and your parents are rich and all, but it never seemed that way. No offense."

"None taken, I didn't know we were rich until this morning. Although, based on what happened to Preston Billings, I'm not sure if we still are."

"This place just reeks of old money. And not in a good way. In a creepy, secret kind of way. If you know what I mean."

"Look, Peter, right now I am so freaked out that everything seems weird. But you're right, we should get out of here and try to find my parents. We'll have dinner, spend the night, and we'll get out of here one way or another in the morning. Sound like a plan?"

"Yeah, that sounds good."

"Hey guys, come on, it's dinnertime!" Dresdale yells from the hall.

"So tell me more," says Aunt Carrie after you have finished the main course of roasted lamb with vegetables. "What happened that all three of you were expelled?"

"Well, it was really unfair--" begins Dresdale before you cut her off.

"I hate to be rude," you say. "But we can't talk about it right now. It is too painful. Thank you so much for this lovely dinner and for putting the three of us up. You have a beautiful house. Have you lived here long?" You know that your attempt to change the conversation is weak, but you are so tired that you don't know what else to do.

"That's too bad, dear," says Aunt Carrie, smiling at you with her mouth only. Her pale blue eyes, much like Dresdale's, stare into yours without blinking. "We can talk about it later. I'm sure the three of you are exhausted, and yes, I have lived here a long time. Although, since Frank passed away it gets a bit lonely. I do have Charles and the rest of the household staff, but it isn't the same as having family. That is why it is such a nice surprise to have you here, Dresdale, and your friends too. The only reason I was asking about the school was that I wanted to see if I could help."

"Thanks, Aunt Carrie. I appreciate it, and the dinner was wonderful."

"I noticed that you did not eat the lamb. Is anything wrong with it?" she asks, looking at Dresdale's plate. The uneaten lamb is half-buried under a pile of mashed potatoes. Dresdale blushes.

"I'm a vegetarian," she says.

"Oh, well. Okay then. Are you sure you had enough to eat?"

"Yes, I'm fine."

"Well, we should be calling your father before dessert. I left him a message that you were here, but he must have been out. You should probably call your mother too."

Once again, Dresdale is unable to get either of her parents on the phone, and the stricken look on her face makes you come out of your own worry for a moment.

"It's okay, Dres," you say. "I'm sure there's a good explanation. Any email from either of them?"

"No. Nothing. This isn't like them. They're never out of touch like this. I'm scared."

You nod and stay silent. You can understand how she feels better than anyone and words seem futile.

"Well, we'll try again in the morning," says Aunt Carrie. "Why don't we have dessert? Clarice made a fruit tart."

You eat the tart in silence. No one says anything. Tension fills the air. Even Aunt Carrie looks upset. She keeps looking at her watch, and she barely touches the tart. You thank Aunt Carrie and head off to bed.

You stare at the elaborate pleated canopy over your bed and think about all that has happened. Sleep seems far away, but your tired body starts to fall asleep when your door bursts open and three men in dark clothes rush into your room.

"Put your hands on your head!" One of them shouts.

Before you can move, two of them grab you and push you onto the floor. You taste carpet. They put handcuffs on you and pull you up roughly to your feet. Someone puts duct tape over your mouth. You try to yell and warn Peter and Dresdale, but all you can do is make moaning sounds.

"Got all three secure, Sarge," says a deep male voice from the hallway. "Positive ID. These are the ones they want."

They take you out of your room and march you down the hall and outside. Aunt Carrie stands by the door. She looks upset, but not surprised. You think you know why.

"You're not going to hurt them!" she says as you are pulled outside. The men holding you don't answer.

They put you in a windowless, small room with a bright light and a table and two chairs. Then you wait for what seems like hours. You desperately need to go to the bathroom, but no one comes to take you to one.

The door opens and two people walk in. One is a tall man with dark hair whom you do not recognize. The other is Dr. Schliemann.

"You may as well tell us everything. Your friends already have," says Schliemann as he walks forward and rips the duct tape off your mouth. You try not to make any noise, but a small cry escapes anyway.

"I haven't done anything!" you say.

"Hardly," says Schliemann with a laugh. "If you confess to your role with the insurgency, it will go easier for you."

"I'm not part of the insurgency," you say, squirming in your chair. You can hardly feel your hands or your arms, they have been held behind you for so long.

"That's not what Preston Billings said."

"I want my lawyer," you answer.

Schliemann laughs again. You feel chilled by the sound. "You have no rights. You have nothing. The only way that you will get out of this room is if you tell me the truth. Begin at the beginning and don't leave anything out. Your friends have already confessed. They told me that you were the leader. The only way out of this room is if I let you go."

"Go to hell!"

"I've already been. It's your turn now."

The End

Ash and Donuts

You grab the wheel of the van and yank it over, and you feel Lucas fighting the new direction. Tires shriek in the wet night. Lucas slams on the brakes, and you slam into your seat-belt. The van shudders and shakes, and you are worried that it will tip over for a moment, but then it settles back down and comes to a stop.

"Oh my god!!"

"I can't breathe!"

"What happened?"

"A moose, I saw a moose," you explain to Lucas Foren, who is looking at you in anger. "It was right on the side of the road, coming toward us. I swear!"

"I didn't see anything," says Foren. He peers into the murky blackness. "But, no harm, no foul. Next time, just let me know when you see something. Don't just grab my wheel."

"There was no time! We were heading straight for it!"

"Okay, okay. Settle down. Everyone all right?"

"Yeah," Peter says. "I'm okay. Just how I like to get woken

up, but I'm fine."

Lucas starts the van up and continues on through the night. Peter takes over driving around 3 AM. "Make sure not to ride the brakes," Lucas says as he heads into the back to take a rest. You stay with Peter as he drives. Since you don't have your license yet, you don't offer to drive. After the moose incident, you don't want to risk anything else, so you watch the road, looking for anything that might be a danger.

Peter drives quickly through the darkness. Since the United States and Provinces took over Mexico and most of Canada, they have said that freedom of movement would be much easier for all. It hasn't worked out that way in reality, but you don't run into any Gatekeeper blockades or impromptu borders. You are thankful for that. The mountains of New Hampshire fade in the distance behind you in the cold light of pre-dawn, and the flat plains leading into Quebec spread before you like a rumpled gray sheet on an old bed.

"Why are we going to Ungava Bay, exactly?" Peter asks as you see the morning glow of Montreal in the distance. The city's glow fades as that of the sun grows stronger.

"Well, that is where Mr. Billings told us to go. My parents were headed there. But I got the feeling it was for more than just the FFA. And, well, that's about it."

"What do you think Rimy can do to help us find your parents? And why did they need all that money?"

"I don't know, Peter, I don't know. I'm so tired and confused, I guess I am just going where I am told."

"Just make sure you know what you are doing before you do it."

"I'll try," you say. "We should stop and take a bathroom

break. Look for the next store you see. I could use a cup of something warm, too."

You stop at a small store and use the restroom. You are on the outskirts of Montreal, but it looks like a city to you. As you are wandering around the chip aisle with a warm cup of hot cocoa in your hands, you hear a loud explosion. Bags of chips tumble to the floor. Windows shatter and you hear people screaming. After a moment, everything goes silent. The three of you stumble outside. A sharp chemical smell is in the air.

Lucas Foren is standing in the parking lot. He has bits of plastic in his hair and on his body. About a block away, you see what used to be a car but is now just a mass of orange and yellow flames. Thick black smoke fountains into the morning air. Ash is all around.

"Get in the van. We have to get out of here. Now."

"What was that?"

"I don't know who did it," responds Foren once you are on the road. "It could have been the FFA attacking the Keepers or the other way around. Either way, we need to get out of here."

"Did you see anyone in the car?" Dresdale asks.

"Nah, I didn't notice it until it blew up. I didn't see anyone, but there must have been someone driving it, at least."

"Two days, two murders. Nobody can find their parents. This is a messed-up world we are living in," Peter says with a dark laugh. You feel nauseous.

No one talks much as you drive the rest of the way toward Ungava Bay.

"How are we supposed to get in touch with this Rimy guy

once we get there?" Foren asks after a while.

"We're supposed to call his 'mom's' house once we get into town. Even though he's supposedly an orphan. Dresdale, did you get a response to the email you sent him before we left New York?"

"Yeah, he said he would get gear ready for us. He didn't say for what though. He did say to prepare for the cold."

"I heard it used to be really cold up there, before the Big Melt," Peter chimes in. "The bay wasn't really used. No one cared about it except for a few Inuit and animals. Then after the Northwest Passage became a reality, they needed a good place to run the shipping from."

"Where'd you learn that from?" Dresdale asks with surprise. "I thought you slept through our Global Climate Change class?"

"Just the boring parts," Peter replies defensively. "I pay more attention than you think!"

The outside temperature drops steadily the farther north you go. You sleep in the van at night when Peter, Dresdale, or Lucas can't drive anymore. In the morning after your third night, you notice that there is a deep frost on the inside of the van's windows. By the time you near Ungava Bay, the van's tired old heating unit is blasting on high, but no heat makes its way to the back. You have never been as cold as you are now, and you haven't even gone outside yet.

"Wake up," Foren says. "We're almost there. You have to give your friend a call and find out where to meet him. Boy, I sure do miss cell phones. They were a pain, but they made life a lot easier sometimes. That alone might make joining the FFA worthwhile."

Ungava Bay spreads out before you in the cold light of late fall. The bay is blue, and you see a flotilla of ships fills the protected harbor. Large tankers and cargo ships compete with small tugs and fishing trawlers for space in the crowded areas near the docks. In the distance, you can see a colony of seals swarming on a small island.

You are relieved to hear Rimy's voice when you call the number in his email. Something familiar amongst all of the new strangeness in your life is comforting.

"I'll bring some stuff when we meet," he says, giving a deep cackle. "Can't say more now. Stay safe. See you soon."

Lucas Foren drives you down to the dock address that Rimy gave you. The blue of the bay is blocked by large, sheet-metal buildings, but they are blue of a different, more homogenous, sort.

"Over here!"

"Rimy!" Peter yells, pointing across Lucas.

Rimy gets you inside the warehouse quickly. He barely acknowledges Dresdale, you, or Peter. You see Peter's shoulders slump in hurt protection. He always retreats inward.

"Who are you?" Rimy asks Lucas Foren. He is not relaxed. Or friendly.

"I'm a friend," Lucas replies with an easy laugh.

"For hire? Who else have you worked for?" Rimy demands.

"Rimy! Listen, I had my doubts," Peter interjects, "but Lucas has done us all right. By my measure, he has come up losing on the costs invested in getting us here. He's the only one who helped us when no one else would."

Rimy looks at Foren and you can see his thoughts clearly on his face: SPY!

"Whatever," Lucas says nonchalantly. "I never expected a parade. Good luck, you three. Watch out for the Keepers. And I hope you find your folks."

"Thanks for your help," Peter says. He looks at Lucas meaningfully. You wonder why. "I really mean it. You were there for us, for me."

"Okay. I guess I gotta go," Foren replies.

Your throat hurts. You don't move an inch. You don't say a word. You force yourself to speak.

"Thank you."

"You're welcome," Foren says as he steps into the van.

You watch him drive away and you think how lucky you have been. If he had been incompetent, evil, or stupid, you would most likely be talking to tall, scary Gatekeepers right now.

"We have to leave now. We don't have time to wait. We need to get to the maelstrom and make our way inside before the weather changes," Rimy announces.

"Make our way inside what?" Dresdale asks.

Rimy pauses and slowly looks at all three of you.

"The Earth, into the inner Earth," he states.

You, Dres, and Peter all exchange looks. Rimy, for all his good nature, is not one for practical jokes. You realize he's serious.

"I thought that stuff was just fairy tales," Dresdale says softly.

Rimy looks at the three of you. "So did many people. Things changed when the Northwest Passage opened up." He

QUEBEC LIBRE
UNGAVA BAY
GREENLAND

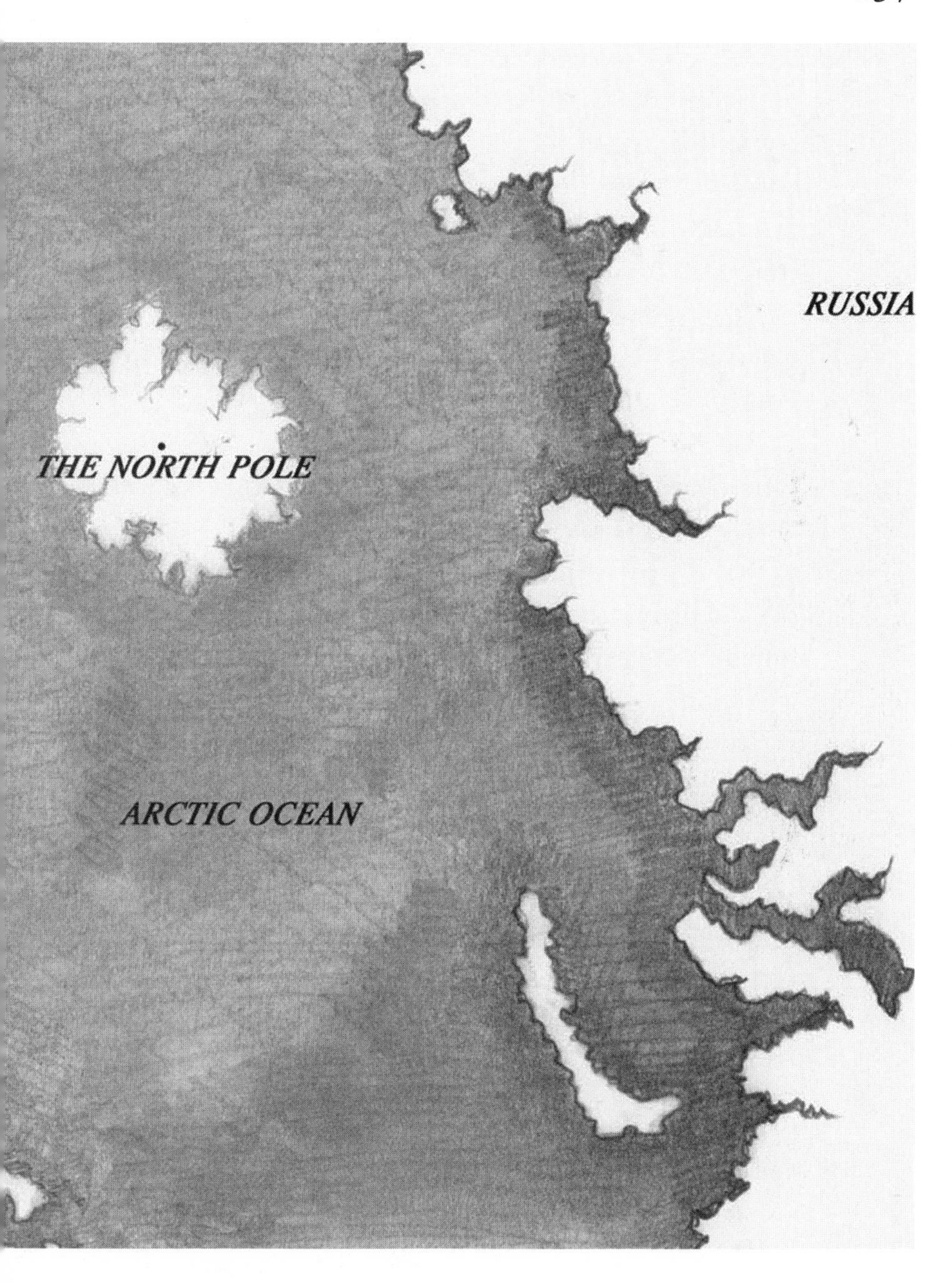
RUSSIA
THE NORTH POLE
ARCTIC OCEAN

pauses again, giving you a chance to absorb the information.

"What's in there? Inside the Earth," you ask.

"That's one of the things your parents were trying to find out," Rimy answers. "But we believe that the US & P government has made contact with someone inside, a leader there who controls an extraordinary energy source," he finishes. "We think it has something to do with recent events here on the outside. With the government's crackdowns and expansions of power."

Rimy disappears into what looks like a warehouse and comes back out almost immediately with a tall man in bright orange rough weather gear.

"We have to leave now to meet the Lemurians," Rimy states. His breath makes frost clouds in the cold air. "Time is running out because of the approaching storm. The Lemurians will know where your parents have been taken, or at least have a good idea."

"Lemurians as in ancient Lemuria, the precursor of Atlantis?" you ask.

"Exactly," Rimy replies curtly. "They are one group we have made positive contact with.This is Captain DeLauriers," he adds by way of introduction to the man in orange. "The Captain's an old and trusted friend of mine and he'll be taking us to the maelstrom."

"Hi, nice to have you with us," the captain says with a faint Quebecois accent. "Rimy says you are good people. We'll be going into some of the roughest seas in the world, and you are going to the roughest spot in them. The maelstrom whirlpool started a couple of years after the polar ice cap finally melted all the way through. No one really knows for sure how it started or what it is going to do, but we do know that it keeps getting bigger and more violent each year. So when we shove off, I need to make sure that you understand how important it is to follow my orders. I won't boss you around unless it is absolutely necessary."

None of you say a word.

"A storm is brewing over near Russia, and it is supposed to hit the pole in the next couple of days," continues the Captain. "We should leave now if we want to get there before the storm. I'll have my crew load your bags from the car and we can get going. Your other gear is already loaded onboard the *Northern Star.*"

"How do we know that my parents are in there?" you demand. "That this is where we should look?"

Rimy looks at you steadily. "I tracked your parents here. They were spotted on the last government craft to depart for the inside. At least we think it was them. We're 99 percent certain."

"What about the $42 million?" you demand. "From my parents' account with Preston Billings. What was that for?"

"To be honest, I have no idea," Rimy replies. "Captain DeLauriers is taking us in place of a Russian tour that canceled."

"Right. No charge for old friends in trouble," the Captain agrees.

You crumble to the ground and clasp your arms around your knees and tuck your head down. It's the same protective position you took as a child when you were hurt or upset.

Everything feels so outlandish, so out of control.

"You okay?" It's Dres. She whispers quietly and puts her hand on your back.

"I'll be okay. Just hurting a bit, is all," you answer. You take a deep breath. "Most people don't know when their life hits a turning point. Mine seems to be in high relief." You try to make smile.

"I don't think we have any choice," Dresdale says quietly. You nod but say nothing.

The three of you help Captain DeLauriers' small crew load fuel and supplies onboard the *Northern Star*. You push off minutes after completing your work. As the lights of Ungava Bay disappear and the thick swell of the open water takes over, you wonder when you will see land again. The thought of an Inner Earth makes you claustrophobic. The only thing keeping panic at bay is the thought you are following after your parents.

After a couple of hours, with the sea spray on your face, it starts to feel good to be on the *Northern Star*. You have the sense that you are actually getting closer to your mom and dad. The *Star* is a small, flat and wide combination boat and hover craft. The Captain tells you that she can hydroplane through heavy chop or glide over pack ice at high speeds. The dual fuel-cell jets are a bit noisy, but at least you know that you are moving fast. After a quick meal, you all go to your tiny bunks and fall asleep. Even Peter's and Rimy's snoring doesn't keep you up.

WRACK!

A loud explosion wakes you up suddenly and you slam your head onto the bunk above you. A bit dazed, you fall out of the bunk and try and get up.

"Stay here," says Rimy. "I'll go see what the problem is."

You rub your head and complain about the pain until Peter tells you to quit whining and let him get back to sleep.

"Bad news," Rimy says as he comes back into the tiny cabin. "The left air jet is blown. Captain DeLauriers says that we need to go back to fix it, but that will take at least two days. Meanwhile, the storm over Russia has picked up and should be at the pole sooner than we thought. We can get by on one engine, but if that goes we would be completely stuck."

You look as usual to your two friends. Dresdale looks confused, and Peter looks like he is sleeping with his eyes open.

"Oh, and one other thing," Rimy says darkly. "The Captain thinks that someone sabotaged the jets. The steel mounting supports on both jets had been weakened. The Captain said repairing the supports on the good engine will be no problem, but that if we are going to turn back, we should do it now."

"Why would they do that?" Peter asks.

"Prevent us from getting too far," Rimy shrugs.

"Come on," says Dresdale. "We'll be fine. I say we go on to the maelstrom and try and beat the storm."

"It's up to you," Rimy says gently. "It's your parents who are missing."

If you decide to turn around, return to Ungava and repair your skimmer, turn to page 155.

If you decide to shove on and continue with one engine so you can beat the coming storm, turn to page 148.

Emerald Bearer

"When will the ritual begin?" you ask, feeling interest verging on fear.

"The ritual can begin in a few moments," Durno says from behind you. It is like an echo. "It is a great honor to be chosen. I myself have never seen the ritual. It is very rare. But do not worry. I swear to you that you will not be harmed. You may even be unharmed."

Unharmed? As if you are harmed to begin with?

Durno's accent is strange to your ears, but you can understand him without straining. Two Lemurians come and lead you away. One is a thin and short male, and the other is a tall female. Both smile at you as they take your arms and lead you away. You see Peter push through people and come toward you.

"Hey! We get to watch, right?" shouts Peter. From the head of the table comes a loud laugh, "We all go to see the ritual," says Sublimas-Chaeko. You notice that his accent is very slight.

Your guides bring you to a small room off the dining hall.

They hand you a robe that glints tones of green in the dim light. The robe feels as soft and light as hummingbird feathers.

They wash your hands, feet, and face with strange herbs. Your face is covered with a chalky paste. The female mimes to you not to try and lick it off, making a funny face to show that you did not want to taste it.

Your escorts take you out into the dining area. It has been completely transformed. Blazing globes pouring out green light stand on top of metal stands set in a circle in the room. All the tables and chairs from the just completed dinner are gone and a glowing disc lies in the middle of the room. A large X cuts the disc into four quarters, and you notice leather bindings set at the ends of the X. As you get nearer to the disc, it starts to glow with the same green light as the globes in the room.

"Get your hands off of me!" Dresdale shouts from behind you. You try to turn and see what is going on, but one of your escorts grabs your head and leads you further toward the now pulsing disc.

"Dresdale, watch out!" Peter yells on the other side of the room. You can see him struggling with three Lemurians. He may be small, but he's tough.

You struggle to get free, but your two guards are strong and they get you into the leather restraints quickly and without hurting you. No matter how you wiggle, you can't get leverage to break free.

The lights go out except for the disc below you, which now seems to be heating up as well as pulsing with the green light. Sublimas-Chaeko stands above you and chants in low Lemurian tones. Sublimas-Chaeko reaches into his robes and

pulls out a shining emerald. The emerald is shaped like a teardrop pin. You squint against the bright light.

He places the emerald in the air directly over your forehead and removes his hand. Instead of falling, the emerald hovers in the air and then slowly rises toward the high ceiling. The emerald's needle tip is pointed straight at you.

"No!" someone yells as the needle drops down at you. It sounds like Rimy.

You squirm as much as possible, but you can't move your head out of the way of the rushing needle. The emerald's point pierces your forehead but you feel no pain.

"Do not fear," says a whisper in your head. "First, tell me who you are?"

"My name is—," you say out loud.

"Your name is not who you are," interrupts the whisper-voice. "Tell me who you are?"

"I don't know who I am, I'm just me, and I'm trying to find my parents and I don't know where I am," you mumble.

"It is enough. We will meet again."

"Wait!" you shout. "Who are you?"

"I am the grower, I am the eroder, I am the water, I am stone, I am the heart, I am many, I am one, the Lemurians call me Orana."

You feel the whisper-voice of Orana slip away, and you also feel your hands, head, and feet being released from the shackles. As soon as your hands are free you reach up to your forehead where there is still a burning and tingling sensation, but you find no wound and no needle made of emerald.

"It went into your forehead," whispers Peter into your ear as he helps you to stand. "There were little ripples of skin around your head where it went in, like it was water."

"Where did it come out?" you ask, feeling the back of your head.

"It didn't," says Peter. He looks scared. "It just went into your head and disappeared."

"I am sorry for frightening you and your friends," Durno says, "but we did not think that you would understand the necessity of how the ritual unfolds. If you feel in any way dishonored or abused, I offer my life as a small repayment of that debt. All of my memories I also offer to you!"

With that, Durno whips off his robe and draws a wicked-looking obsidian knife. He hands it to you hilt first, kneels down, closes his eyes and lifts his head up to expose his pallid throat.

"It's okay," you mutter while fumbling awkwardly with the knife.

"What is going on in this crazy place?" says Peter. "Don't kill the guy, but that was the creepiest thing that I have ever seen! They put a needle in your brain!"

"No, really, Peter, it's okay. I think this will help us find my parents, or at least it didn't hurt me. I'm not sure what it did. A voice spoke to me. And then it went away. Right now, I just want to go to sleep!"

"Come with me," says Rimy. He grasps one hand, and takes the knife gently from your other. You don't remember anything else after that.

You dream of a sometimes dry valley, deep and cool. It is your home. You are late again, but you don't know for what. The small rock farmhouse is in front of you. You pull at the door, but the lock is firm. "Mama! Open the door!! They are coming for me! Mama! Papa!"

"Wake up!" Durno shouts in your ear. "Wake up! We have

to go. The Agarthans have attacked us. We have to leave now."

You see other red-robed and helmeted Lemurians waking Dresdale and Peter. Dressing as quickly as possible, and grabbing the small pack that holds your few possessions, you look around the room to see if you forgot anything.

"Where's Rimy?" You ask Durno.

"He's gone," replies Durno. "He was meeting with Sublimas-Chaeko and the war council when the attack came. The Agarthans targeted the council. We aren't sure if they were killed, captured, or escaped. We don't have time for this, we have to go now!"

"We can't leave Rimy!" says Dresdale, grabbing your arm.

"It is death to go near the council room. Don't throw your life away! The Agarthans have unleashed their Wyrm Hounds. We will die here if we stay any longer!" Durno says, motioning to the other Lemurians to leave the room.

He turns his back on you and goes to the door.

"Are you coming or not?" he asks.

If you decide to try and rescue Rimy, turn to page 110.

If you follow Durno, turn to page 173.

Iced

"Normally I wouldn't risk it, but we know that there is a storm coming," you say. " Someone back in Ungava Bay doesn't want us getting there, or worse. Captain DsLauriers, can you have someone monitoring the remaining jet so we will know to turn back if it acts up?"

"De rien. No problem. We'll get you there safe and sound." Rimy nods his agreement.

"Okay," you say, looking at your watch. "It is 3:30 AM. We should all get back to sleep."

"Oh yeah," says Peter, while Dresdale merely yawns and nods.

You are sleepy, and your head hurts from slamming it into the bunk, but you decide to go out and check the remaining jet. The cold wind is a shock to you as you head out onto the deck and you are thankful for your parka. The skimmer seems to be moving with no problem, and the jet's roar is as loud as before.

While you stand outside, you see flickers of red and green out of the corner of your eye. You blink to clear your eyes, and then you know you are seeing the aurora borealis or Northern Lights. After a long time watching the pulsing colors, you head back into the warmth of the cabin.

Entering the cabin and its warmth, you are overwhelmed by the loss of your parents. Where are they? you wonder. Rimy was supposed to be bringing you answers, but you feel as if you are farther away from your goal than ever before.

"Are you okay?" Dresdale asks. "Do you want to talk about it?"

"I just don't know what to do," you say with a deep sigh. "But I do need to get some sleep. Thanks, though."

"G'nye."

When you wake up for breakfast (smoked salmon and hard rye bread), it is still dark outside the porthole windows. As you go further north, there will be less and less sunlight at this time of year.

"We have made excellent time, even with the blown jet," Capt. DeLauriers announces as he comes into the cabin. "And it looks like the storm will hold off for a bit longer and give us the time to set up the capsule."

"Great," says Peter. "What exactly are we going to be doing with the capsule, anyway?"

"We are going to be measuring the maelstrom from inside it, but don't worry, we'll be completely safe," says Rimy with a smile.

Capt. DeLauriers snorts. "Whatever you say, Rimy."

"Who's burning the bacon?" Dresdale asks.

"That's not bacon! It smells like burning electronics or cables or something," says Peter, looking at Dresdale in disbelief.

"How am I supposed to know? I don't eat the stuff. Help me find where it is coming from," she replies, sniffing at the air to find the source of the smoke.

The smoke starts to really come out, and you all look to its source. Smoke is leaking out of the command cabin where the pilot controls the skimmer. You feel the door, and since it feels cool, you decide to open it. The pilot, Jean, is still in there.

"Stay back!" you yell as you yank the door open.

Smoke rushes out, and you can barely make out the form of Jean slumped on the floor. Captain DeLauriers rushes in and starts spraying the fire extinguisher at the control panel. Dresdale opens the hatches in the main cabin to let in fresh air.

"Is he breathing?" Someone yells out.

"Yeah, yeah, he's breathing," you shout back.

Captain DeLauriers grabs Jean's legs while you get his head. You carry him out into the main cabin. Peter keeps spraying the fire extinguisher, and Rimy rummages through the bulkheads for the medical kit. Jean coughs and writhes on the cabin floor, but the color of his face looks better.

"There is an oxygen tank in the bulkhead above you, Rimy," says the Captain. "If you look after Jean, I'll go check the control cabin. You can stop spraying everything, Peter."

"Oh, right," he says, putting the extinguisher down.

Jean starts to come around once Rimy gets the oxygen mask on him. He begins to talk, but the coughing comes back. Dresdale hands him a glass of water.

"It just went 'pop,'" he finally coughs out. "No warning."

"Bad news. The whole main electronics system is fried," says the Captain, rejoining you. "I only have enough fuel in the backup hover system to get us maybe ten kilometers. We can perch ourselves on an iceberg and try and repair the skimmer out here, or anchor it and take the lifeboat back to Ungava. Luckily, we have plenty of food, but it would be a long and slow journey back."

"How long will it take to repair the electronics system?" You ask.

"Normally I would say twelve to eighteen hours, but since we have had two failures already, I would want to check out the whole ship, and that will take longer. Remember, a huge storm is supposed to hit before long. We don't want to be powerless when that hits. Both the lifeboat and the *Northern Sta*r have distress beacons. I have already activated the *Star's*."

"How close are we to the maelstrom?" Asks Dresdale quietly, as she cradles Jean's head in her hands.

"Pretty close, about forty kilometers," answers the Captain.

"Rimy, can the capsule move?"

"Limited, but we could maybe make it to the maelstrom. What are you thinking, Dresdale?"

"We need to get off the *Northern Star,* or at least camp on a larger iceberg. How about we use the research capsule to continue on our way? We're almost there."

"It's risky, but this whole operation is risky. After what happened to Preston, I don't think we can afford to wait around to be rescued," you say.

"I've got a bad feeling about this," says Peter as you climb into the capsule.

The capsule is a long, large black tube, with molded sensor mounds placed periodically all over its surface. It appears to be made of steel, but when you touch it with your bare hand, it doesn't get stuck.

"Get onboard!" Rimy shouts. "We've gotta go!"

You try to strap into one of the four couches, but Dresdale has to help you with the six-point harness. Peter and Rimy are in the front of the tube, peering out of the small windshield into the darkness of perpetual night.

The leads and pack ice that you had just been jetting over on the *Northern Star* take much more time and effort to get over in the capsule. The bottom of the capsule has a dual tread system, and the treads act like paddles in the softer ice and water areas. The going is slow, but you can tell you are making progress.

There is little pack ice in the Arctic ocean since the Big Melt, but this far north still seems like a forbidding and cold place.

"We are getting near the maelstrom," says Rimy after a long period of silence in the capsule. "You can hear the rushing of the water and the ice now."

As you get nearer to the maelstrom, Rimy lets out a low whistle.

"What?" Peter asks. "What's wrong?"

"The maelstrom has increased in power since the last time I was here. That might present a problem with our getting through to the passage. However, we don't have any choice this time, as we don't have enough fuel to make it back to the *Northern Star*. We'll be safe enough."

"What's 'enough.'" mutters Peter.

Rimy takes the capsule and drives it straight into the black pool of water that surrounds the maelstrom whirlpool. The roar of the swirling water drowns out your conversation as you submerge into it. Rimy turns on a powerful spotlight, and you see the shape of the gigantic funnel slicing through the blackness straight ahead of you.

As soon as the nose of the capsule touches the edge of the funnel, it yanks you to the right as if a train had hit it. Once inside the maelstrom, you twist and turn as you spin ever faster downward. The capsule starts to screech louder than the maelstrom, and you can feel the vibrations rocking through your body. Without warning, a section of the ceiling comes loose and smashes into your leg.

The pain makes you gasp, but you still yell out. "Pull the emergency cord!"

Something crashes into your head, and you fall into the swirling blackness.

When you wake up, you see that your broken leg is being held up by traction wires. Your head feels like it is stuffed with cotton candy, but you manage to croak out.

"Where are my parents?"

Dresdale leans over you and says, "We'll find them, but first you need to rest. Peter and Rimy are fine, but the capsule is toast."

You close your eyes and fall back into darkness.

The End

Truth or Dare

"The last thing I want to do is turn around. Every moment in this search counts. But I don't think we should risk being completely stranded," you announce.

Everyone nods. You think Peter looks relieved but you aren't sure.

The return trip passes quickly, even with only one jet. Captain DeLauriers immediately gets to work repairing the other. He also checks every other bit of machinery on the *Northern Star*. He reports that he found a small charge in the electrical system. The Captain does not once leave the warehouse where the Star is being worked on. When you finally relaunch, he looks exhausted.

"Are you going to be all right?" you ask.

"I'll be fine. When I was younger we would fish for four days straight when the salmon were running. This is nothing," he says with a grin as he moves into the control cabin.

With both engines on full throttle, the trip to the maelstrom passes by like a bumpier and noisier train voyage.

Looking out the porthole, you spy the hulking shapes of polar bears every now and then, but you are moving so fast it is hard to see what they are doing. You think that a dark shape with a rounded head rising out of the dark water is a harp seal, but you can't be sure.

"It's time to prepare the capsule," says Rimy.

"I'll get you in as close as possible," Captain DeLauriers shouts over the wind, "but I have to watch out for those chunks of ice that are ripped from the pack ice. You'll need to wade into the maelstrom proper on your own. How long do you think you'll need?"

"We're not coming back," replies Rimy softly.

"What are you talking about?" asks the Captain.

"I didn't tell you before, because we need your utmost trust," Rimy says to the Captain, who looks skeptical. "Our scientists feel the maelstrom is a one-way entrance now. With all the flow of water going into it, there is no way to navigate back out. When we return to the surface, it will be through a different exit."

"You know, Rimy," replies the Captain with a laugh. "I knew you were up to something else all along. I was just being polite by not bringing up all the holes in your story. I'll get the capsule ready."

Strapped securely in place, you watch the water outside the capsule through the porthole. There isn't much to see in the darkness of night and water, but there is a lot to feel. Each time

Rimy adjusts the capsule with its external fins, you feel the different threads of currents tearing in all directions. The prevailing sensation is one of falling. If you weren't so nervous it would be fun.

"Depth is now 6,000 meters, and we're going down fast!" says Dresdale through the intercom. "We're in the Eurasian basin, the deepest part of the Arctic Ocean! That is lower than the lowest point."

"What was that?" Peter shouts, as a squealing and wrenching sound blasts you from all sides.

"The steering fins can't handle the pressure and the stress; don't worry, they are made to break away without causing damage," Rimy replies.

While still spinning, you don't seem to be circling around

in broad scope as much. If you weren't facing straight down, it would feel as though you were standing still. You look over at Peter and you see that he has passed out. A thin line of drool is coming out of his mouth and it swings rapidly from all the spinning, but at least you can see that he is breathing.

"Peter is out!" you yell.

Dresdale opens her eyes and looks at you, but she can't do much more. Rimy seems to be lost in a trance. You can't control the path of the capsule any longer, so what is the point of worrying? But you worry a little anyway. You see the depth gauge hit 18,000 meters and then you feel a great weight pushing down on you, everything goes white and black at the same time and you pass out.

When you wake up, you feel like you are still spinning, but soon you realize you have stopped. All you feel is a slight wave motion and a gentle touch on your head.

"Are you okay?" Dresdale asks, lifting your head.

You open your eyes, startled by light slipping in through the portholes. The light is weak and reddish, but after the permanent night of the Arctic, it still makes you blink.

"Where are we?" Peter asks, voicing what you are thinking.

"We made it," says Rimy. "But the journey was very difficult. I don't think I would try that route again."

"You didn't answer the question, Rimy," says Peter.

"He's pretty good at that," quips Dresdale.

"Noted, Dresdale. I'll try to be more forthcoming in the future," Rimy answers. "We are in the Blood Sea of Agartha, one of the kingdoms, now an empire, of the Inner Earth. I am going to see if we can get to a hideout of some Lemurian refugees that helped me previously. They know of your parents," Rimy says, looking at you. "I'm hoping they can help lead us in the right direction."

"Let's get moving then!" you say.

Rimy nods and gets the capsule ready. He deploys a secondary set of steering fins and a small turbine. Unfortunately, the emergency flotation system was used in the maelstrom, so you won't be able to use the capsule as a submarine.

"Can we breathe the air?" Peter asks, looking out at the red sea and the red clouds roiling above you.

"Yes, but you may find it different, and also the water, too. Things here are more than a bit odd. The Lemurians look basically human, but they aren't, quite. To be honest, I've always thought they looked a bit like solid ghosts," Rimy says, trailing off at the end. "Ah, land ahead!"

The land in front of you is rocky and barren, and you have a hard time figuring out where Rimy is taking you. Waves splash against the red rocks, and you want to yell to Rimy that you are getting too close. Just as you are about to yell out, you see that there is a gap between two thin towers of rock. Rimy calmly pilots the capsule between the rocks and docks it.

"So, you've been here before," Dresdale says, inspecting the dock. "It looks like the water has been rising. See how it's lapping over the dock."

"Just be careful," says Rimy, looking at Dresdale. "The Lemurians are expecting us, but they have to be very cautious. Sceptus almost wiped them out."

"Sceptus?" you ask. "Who's Sceptus?"

"He's the emperor of Agartha. And the cause of this whole mess," Rimy grunts.

"Over there," whispers Peter, pointing to a tunnel entrance with a camouflaged red door.

Four orange robed figures emerge slowly from the entrance. The figure in front makes hand gestures, and the three others come forward toward the capsule.

"Smile!" breathes Rimy as he waves at the figures.

You don't feel like smiling, but you do anyway. The way that the figures move makes you feel nervous. You smell death.

"Rimy!" says a normal-sounding male voice from the first figure. He pushes back the hood of his robe and reveals a whitish-red face mostly covered by a mirrored eye shield.

"Durno!" Rimy replies, smiling at his Lemurian friend. Rimy keeps speaking, but you don't understand anything else he says. Bits sound like ancient Greek and Latin, but mostly they talk in a language that sounds alien to you. Puellea? Cosmosis? Politikis? What are they saying? Everything sounds a bit familiar, but still a bit off.

While Rimy and Durno talk, the other three Lemurians come over and help you, Dresdale and Peter down from the capsule. They also hand you drink pouches. You drink of the cool nectar and you feel your spirits lift, if only just a bit.

"Hello," says Peter brightly as he follows along the rock dock. "You don't have any showers here, do you?"

His escort replies, but no one can tell what he is saying. The three of you follow your guides into the tunnel. Once inside, they take off their robes and face-masks. Pale, but not albino, for there is no red tinge to their skin once out of the light, they look like humans, but with long fingers and skin that seems to be composed of solidified mist. You shiver without knowing why.

"Looks like a military camp," says Dresdale, indicating the piles of supplies stacked in the tunnel entrance. Most of the stacks are nautical in nature: ropes, sails, grease. But there are also a few steel rods with nasty-looking blades on the ends.

"Yeah, those things aren't guns," you say, looking at the steel rods with the blades. "But they look lethal anyway."

"Where has Rimy taken us?" Peter asks, but nobody answers him.

You are led to a windowless room hewn out of the red rock that is most of what you have seen besides the inner sea. A table with a ceramic water pitcher and some crumbly cheese on a plate has been set up in the center of the room. Several chairs, one small bed, and a thin blue rug are in the room. Glowing dimly on the low ceiling is a strip of phosphorescent paint on the rough rock. The paint gives you almost enough light to see clearly, but not quite.

Your guides point to an alcove in the corner and mime washing their faces and eating and drinking.

"We get the picture," says Peter, and the Lemurians leave the room, closing the odd-looking door behind them.

"Do you think it's locked?" Dresdale asks.

"Only one way to find out," says Peter trying the handle. It moves easily, and the door opens a few inches. You see the face of one of your guides looking back at you through the open crack. Peter smiles at him and closes the door.

"Well, it isn't locked, but someone is keeping an eye on us," you say while moving toward the table with the refreshments.

There is no shower, but the alcove has a sophisticated privy and a wash basin that just uses gentle vibrations of air to dislodge dirt and grime off of your hands. Dresdale has to threaten Peter to stop playing with it so she can use the facilities.

Rimy joins the three of you after about an hour or so. He looks pleased with himself as he walks into the room and pours himself a mug of water.

"Why are we being kept prisoner?" you ask Rimy before he can take his first sip.

"We aren't really prisoners; they just have to be careful with us. Anyway, we have been invited to dinner with the head of this camp. There's no direct correlation in our language, but he is sort of a combination general and judge. His name is Sublimas-Chaeko and he has been responsible for resisting Emperor Sceptus and the armies of Agartha along the Long Coast of the Inner Sea," Rimy says, taking his sip of water. "He might be someone who can help find your parents. At least I hope so."

Peter naps, Dresdale makes notes in her journal, and Rimy meditates in one of the chairs. You pace around the room. Finally someone comes and tells you to come for dinner.

The dinner itself is amazing, forty types of strange mushrooms that you have never seen, some cut thick like juicy steaks, others as small as grains of rice and almost as starchy. Rimy glares at the three of you, but he does not stop you from trying the glasses of wine that your hosts pour. You begin to feel a little funny, so you switch to water.

After you are done eating, Sublimas-Chaeko stands up and makes a speech. He is dressed in a long robe that drapes his body like flowing silver. You all listen absently to the nonsense words until Rimy gives an audible gasp. Luminastis. Eternastis. Oraclis.

Sublimas-Chaeko looks over at Rimy and repeats what he just said. Rimy replies sharply in Lemurian. The two of them glare at each other after a long and heated discussion. At the end, Rimy turns his head and looks directly at you. "We have a problem. They want you to participate in their Truth Enlightenment Ritual."

"Sure," Dresdale says. "It sounds interesting. What is it?"

"Not you, Dres," Rimy replies. "He specifically wants you."

"Me?" you ask. You take a breath and shrug.

"And I can't really tell you what it is or whether there are harmful effects. There is much more that I don't know about this inner world than what I do know," says Rimy.

"As long as it is nothing dangerous, I don't mind," you say, thinking it came out bravely, but you are wary. "But why me? If you don't mind asking."

"Sublimas says that you created a resonance with one of the compound's guardian Emerald crystals. And that you will be given a great honor if you agree to participate," Rimy continues. "I told him I would ask you, but not compel you, to perform the ceremony."

"It seems kind of touchy-feely to me," sniffs Peter. "'Truth Enlightenment Ritual' sounds like a cult."

"You should know before you make your decision that they said you would be 'bonded' to the Emerald network," Rimy says, staring at you. "Do you trust them?" you ask.

"I know Durno, and he has always seemed trustworthy, but I have never met Sublimas-Chaeko before," is Rimy's answer.

"Will it do anything to help me find my parents?" you ask.

Rimy shakes his head. "Sublimas says that they have neither seen nor heard anything."

If you agree to participate in this strange ritual, turn to page 142.

If you decline the Lemurian's offer, and decide to continue to search for information on your parents, turn to page 66.

Burning Rope

You cast a glance at your two friends.

"We'll go with you. It's the best chance to find my parents," you say.

"There are no guarantees," Maggie replies.

You nod.

"We have to leave now," Harry repeats. "They'll have tracked the shard to this place, and sunset will be our best chance to sneak into the cave complex." Harry opens the door, waving you out of the storage unit. Neila has climbed back into his trunk and Maggie is carrying it with some difficulty. You follow them, not knowing if this was the best choice or your only one.

"We'll take Maggie's truck and meet up with François. He should be done with his chase by now," Harry directs.

"Here, I'll help you," Peter says to Maggie, taking hold of the small trunk. You hear a buzz from inside the box that you suppose is a positive sound. You think of purring crickets trying to sing like birds. The sky is dark red at the horizon, and the sun is about to disappear as you pull up to the entranceway to Carlsbad Caverns. Maggie pulls over about a mile away from the edge of town, and François comes running from behind a sage bush and hops into the truck.

"Schliemann closed down the evening public bat shows, but it will still be a good time to try and sneak in. When a couple of hundred thousand bats are flying around, it is hard to pay attention to anything else," she explains.

"Maggie is right," François says, "but we still need to be careful as we get close to the entrance. Schliemann and his goons found most of the secret tunnels that we used to get access to the caves. He doesn't know about the one leading to the Bell Cord Room. Yet."

You have memorized most of the caverns and can picture the Bell Cord Room in you mind. It is named that because of the stalactite coming through a hole in the ceiling that looks like a bell pull hanging down.

"The Bell Cord is near the Left-Hand Tunnel, the deepest known location of the--"

"We know all of this," Peter interrupts, "we spent all of last summer exploring the caves."

"Well," François responds, turning in his seat to stare Peter in the eye, "if you know so much, why don't you tell me how to access the secret tunnel to the Bell Cord Room?"

Peter just glares.

"He does have you there," Dresdale chimes in. She gets a glare as well.

"Right," says Maggie, all business as she calmly drives off the side of the road onto an old dirt fire road. She smoothly shifts into four-wheel drive and tells you about the security measures taken by Schliemann.

"It is more like an armed fort than a research facility at this point," she begins. "I don't know where Schliemnan gets his power, but it is real. Hundreds of people are here now. We think they have discovered the volcanic tube network leading to the land where Neila and his people are from. He says his people are messengers, and that there are special ways that they can traverse the barriers that are not available to humans or other non-Illuminated. The tube network is extremely valuable."

"Why is it so valuable?" Dresdale asks.

Neila answers from within the trunk. His voice is faint but clear.

"The inner world will bring the answer to your search for the answers to your problems. Can you please let me out of this trunk?"

"'Answers to your problems.' That sounds pretty vague."

"Regardless," Maggie continues as François lets Neila out of the trunk. His glow lights up the interior of the cabin until he pulls a tawny cloak out and covers up until he no longer gives off light. "Schliemann thinks it is important as well. It isn't just us. We need to get Neila past the volcanic tube entrance to his transport portal."

"I will ride the energy home," Neila says from his deep hood.

"We will try and sneak in there, and then come back for your parents. We are much more likely to run into trouble then. That is why we will send Neila and his friends home first. Schliemann has lots of personnel, including armed guards. François will do the sneaky stuff and we will be backup. Our only chance is stealth and superior knowledge of the caves. We're here."

Harry, quiet until this point, grabs your hand as he climbs into the vacated drivers' seat of the truck. "Good luck. I'll be here, ready to get you and your parents out of here when you get back."

François gives you all caving gear, and Maggie leads you in silence through the scrub desert. "Keep the headlights off until we are inside, and no talking!" Streams and clumps of bats fly through the darkening sky. Most are Mexican Freetails, but you know there are other kinds mixed in. You figure that you have hiked about a mile or so when François signals you to stop. He drops into a dark hole and disappears. Maggie follows, as do Dresdale and Peter. Peter is carrying the limp form of Neila.

You've spent lots of time in caves over the past six months, and you have never felt claustrophobia, but something about this dark hole brings out fears that pulse and pound. Ignoring them, you jump in the hole. You belly-crawl in the dark for quite a ways before you see François turn on his headlamp.

"Only a bit further," he whispers, "and then it opens up and we will join Neila's companions, Alegna and Setrips."

You come to a larger room and you see the familiar soda

straw stalactites hanging from the ceiling. The air is moist and cool, and the whole, otherworldly site is made even odder by the glowing friends of Neila crouching over a steaming pot.

"I'll let you down! Stop squirming!" Peter says as he puts Neila down. Neila runs to his friends and they all hug each other at the same time.

You move on after the reunion, with François and Maggie's urging.

Normally you would have loved to explore and just soak in the amazing caves that you travel through, but you don't have time. Your parents need you.

"There is a long drop ahead. I will belay you and let you down, one by one. From there is only a short ways until the Left-Hand Tunnel. Absolutely no talking."

You spin as you drop into the cave below, and light from your headlamp makes shadows dance and jump around. Everyone else but you is on the floor of the cave below, waiting, except for François above. You are only about eight or ten feet off the floor when there is a blinding flash of light and roar of wind. The rope lowering you breaks, and you fall.

"Oh my god! What is it?" Peter yells. You gasp and writhe on the sandy floor of the cave, blinded by the flash.

You blink your eyes to clear them as you sit up. Looking across to cave, you see a burning man shape. It glows a baleful red-orange in the darkness. You feel heat on your face.

"Radiant Ones!" Neila yells. "Run!"

In one smooth motion, Peter swoops down and picks up Neila and runs in the opposite direction of the burning shape walking toward you. Glowing footprints of molten rock and sand mark the creature's path. You stand stunned for a moment before running away as quickly as possible. Unlike Peter, you do not stop to pick up an Illuminatee. Their small legs can't keep up with you, or the Radiant One, and they fall behind.

"Follow me!" Maggie shouts. "The lab complex is right ahead."

You hear high-pitched screams of pain and terror, and you see Peter trying to hold onto the struggling Neila as he runs. With the orange glow behind you, you round the corner to the large cavern where the lab complex is. This is where your parents are being kept. All of the buildings are on fire.

"NO!!!!" you scream as smoke billows up toward the high ceiling of the cavern. Already it is hard to see, with your headlamp illuminating cone-shaped sections of thicker and lighter smoke.

You see Gatekeepers with rifles rush toward the glowing figure of a Radiant One standing in the ruins of the lab buildings.

"Fire!" yells the Gatekeeper in charge. The Gatekeepers fire their rifles at once. Without seeming to notice the effect of bullets ripping into its body, the Radiant One turns to the uniformed Gatekeepers. In three swift moves, it grabs a Gatekeeper, picks him up, and throws his burning body at the others.

"Keep moving," Peter yells as he grabs your arm. Dresdale is with him, and he is cradling Neila in his arms like a child.

"Where?"

"Away from these burning freaks!" he shouts as he pulls you into a thick wall of smoke. Choking on the fumes, you rush forward, banging your knees and shins, but making good time.

"Neila says his transport site is only a little further on. If we can get him there he can contact home and warn them."

The noise of the battle raging behind you recedes as you travel deeper into the cave system. You are in shock. Your parents were in the building that was burning. That was what Maggie told you.

"Where's Maggie!"

"I don't know," Dresdale says, turning to look at you. "Do you know where Neila's friends are?"

A spasm of guilt makes you heart hurt. "I think they're dead. One of the burning things caught them."

"Oh."

"Little ways," Neila whispers to Peter. "I will show."

Neila stands and moves toward a massive stalagmite in the center of the small cave. It is much taller than the small being. Neila begins to sing, and then he reaches out his glowing hand and touches the crystal stalagmite. It begins to glow and pulse the same color as Neila. He sways and gives a soft moan.

"Much news," Neila says, stepping away from the crystal. The glow stops. Neila looks at you. "Child of the child, your parents have been taken in."

"What? What are you talking about?"

"The Radiant Ones were waked by passage to the inner world. Parents no longer here. You come inside as well. It is the only way. The Radiant Ones is death. I am too weak to travel by crystal. We will have to take the path that has been opened."

"I think I hear them coming," Peter whispers. Dresdale tugs at your sleeve.

"Come on, let's go," you say, putting your exhaustion and fear aside.

Continued on page 33 of The Golden Path
Volume II: Burned By The Inner Sun

Bram Interious

Running after Durno, you, Peter, and Dresdale try and keep up with the Lemurians. You struggle, despite being in good shape from soccer practice. The ground is uneven and rocky, but Durno and his two companions seem to flow over the ground, cloudlike.

Pushing yourself, you sprint ahead and speak with Durno. "Where are we going?" you gasp.

"Don't waste your wind talking. We are going to the capital of Lemuria. Light Home City would be the closest translation in your tongue," Durno says without breaking stride. "Chew on these herbs. It will give you energy. Save some for your friends."

You take the small bundle of herbs like a baton in a relay race. They smell and taste bitter, but immediately you feel a small burst of energy. Slowing down, you let Peter and Dresdale catch up with you.

"Oh, this is a type of ephedra," Dresdale says when you

hand it to her. She pauses and tries to catch her breath before continuing. "You know, ma huang? Morman tea? Anyway, it should give us a burst of energy, but don't eat too much, it can make you sick."

"You're amazing, Dres," Peter says. You are not sure if he is making fun of her or not.

"Shut up and run!" Durno hisses in your ear.

The red sun is obscured by thick clouds that threaten to rain, but never do. You fall into the mind dead rhythm of running. The pain you feel in your legs and chest is the only thing you can concentrate on. Thoughts and worries of your parents fade away as you continue to scramble along.

Dresdale turns her ankle on a shifting rock but grits her teeth and continues on. Peter gets sick, but he too keeps going. Durno passes a skin of water around. You don't know how long you run; it seems an eternity.

"Stop! We've made it to our hideout. Just in time. A mud storm is brewing. Can you hear that?!" Durno demands.

You strain but hear nothing.

A tall rocky cliff, reddish in color, confronts you. Durno and the other two Lemurians approach the cliff face and examine it closely and expertly.

"Peter!" He is scrubbing at something on his shirt. You try not to think about what it probably is. "You know a lot about geology, why not help Durno?"

"I'll try," Peter responds. "The cliff looks like a big chunk of basalt, but there are different types of rock over that way."

You sit and watch the Lemurians as they search for the entranceway. Why can't they find the door to their own place?

You hear a rushing sound, very distant.

"Is that it?" you cry. "That low whoosh?"

"Yes, we must hurry," Durno says. He sounds even more nervous than he did when you escaped.

"Eureka!" Peter cries out. The three Lemurians go over and look at what he has found. They look closely at the rock, visors up and faces twisted by squinting. Durno reaches out and pushes three of his fingers into small depressions on the rock. You hear a loud click, and a tiny crack appears at the bottom of the cliff face. A narrow passage, no more than two feet wide opens in front of Durno and Peter.

"Cool," Dresdale comments. "Did you see how tight that seal was?"

You have to take off your backpack to fit into the passage, as well as having to crouch down so that your head does not scrape against the rough ceiling. You notice that Durno and the two other Lemurians crouch in the passageway.

After a hundred yards, the passage takes a hard right turn, goes for a few more yards, and opens into a small room with a stone table and benches. Two lights glow dimly red in sconces on the walls. A wash basin and four bunk beds covered with a mossy covering fill the room.

"Look at that detail," Dresdale murmurs, pointing to the table and the benches. "I've never seen stonework so fine. I should know; I studied sculpture."

"Yeah, for one semester," Peter chirps. "That usually makes someone an expert, right?"

Dresdale gives him a black look.

You turn your attention away from your friends and back

to the room. The stone of the tabletop reflects the dim red light like a darkened mirror. Small engravings of fantastical creatures adorn the backs of both benches. Strange writing accompanies the carvings.

"Did the Lemurians make this hideout, Durno?" Dresdale asks.

Durno pauses from unpacking his bag and looks at Dresdale. "No, this space was carved by the Kandaru, or Troglodytes. Once ancient enemies before the Sphere War, they are now our closest ally against the legions of Sceptus. The Troglodytes can do things with stone that no others can. That's why we had such a hard time finding the door."

"I believe it," Peter says, looking at the built-in oven with an intricately carved flue.

"Get comfortable. We'll be here for several days at least. We're lucky we made it. If you listen, you can hear the start of the mudstorm."

"What's a mudstorm? I've never heard that term before," Dresdale asks.

Moments later you hear a loud THWACK! And feel the stone about you shudder and shift.

"There. It just hit," Durno replies. "They used to be quite rare, but they've become more and more frequent in the last thirty years or so. Ever since the sun started to grow brighter. The weather here in the inner world is similar to that of the surface world, or so Rimy explained. I have never been to outer Earth myself. However, we have always had a semi-regular series of dust storms that scoured the lands of the inner world. These storms would bury farms and choke animals, but they also prevented the sun from heating the whole land to the point where life would be impossible."

"So how do the mudstorms happen, are they related to the dust storms?" Dresdale queries. She is so excited that she begins to chew her fingernails.

"Yes," Durno replies, impressed with Dresdale. "When a dust storm on the other side of the world gets too large, particles of dust get flung with such force into the inner atmosphere that they pass out of the gravitational well on one side and get pulled into the other side. Usually it just falls as dust, and we deal with it since the fallen dust acts as good soil. But when the waves of dust encounter a strong storm system, the circular motion of the storm brings the dust and water together and concentrates it. Listen!"

You hear a thick splatting sound and picture streams of mud falling from the sky.

"Doesn't sound too bad," Peter offers, helping himself to the fried treats the Lemurians prepared while Durno was talking.

"Try breathing when there is no air, only mud," Durno says. "Everything is slippery in a mudstorm, and you can't see. If you fall down, you'll be covered and drowned in a matter of minutes. We're lucky to be here."

The mudstorm lasts for two days. You feel trapped. You dream of your parents being held in a dark jail. Your mother begs you to bring water. No matter what you do, they are always beyond your reach. You wake many times during the night even though the moss-filled beds are surprisingly comfortable and dry.

The two other Lemurians with Durno are Turina and Keldso. They are brother and sister and the niece and nephew of Durno. The language barrier makes it difficult to communicate. You finally resort to a Lemurian form of chess to pass the time. Dresdale and Peter play cards all day long, mainly Gin Rummy. Dresdale wins most of the games. You ask Peter why he keeps playing, and he tells you, "One of these days, I'll figure her out, and then watch who's doing the winning!"

You spend a lot of time in the passageway, down by the door, waiting for the mudstorm to pass.

"You know," Dresdale says, startling you. "At least you know that your parents love you and want you with them. They may be gone right now, but no matter where they are, they still love you."

"Of course they love me," you respond, not knowing what Dresdale means. "They're my parents; that's their job!"

"Well, some parents do their job better than others," replies Dresdale.

"What does that mean?" you ask.

"Haven't you ever wondered why you've never met my parents?"

"Of course I have," you say, lying. "You always say they're too busy with work. At least that's what you told me when they missed the Spring Play."

"It's true, you know? They're too busy, but they've always been too busy. Dad is busy saving people's lives on the operating table, while Mom is too busy working on her latest case to even know that I'm gone. Why do you think they let me work on the excavation at Carlsbad? It was a relief for them that neither of them had to deal with me for the summer. Why do you think I went to English boarding school when I was five? Do you think any kid wants to leave home when they are five?"

"I'm sorry," you say, not lying. "I guess I never have really thought about it."

"Look, I wouldn't have brought it up, but maybe you should think beyond your own problems. We all came along to help you. Maybe you should ask Peter how he's doing? He's been an orphan his whole life. Think about that."

You watch Dresdale walk down the passageway and to the main room, with its light and company. You hear Peter's high-pitched laugh, but you are not ready to join them. Not yet. She's right, but you're not ready. Not yet.

Durno wakes you on the morning of the third day. You are glad to be awake. Your dreams were filled with people yelling at you that you had to hurry, that you had no time and that you needed to do it NOW!

"The storm has passed. Now we see what it has done," Durno announces. He mutters a few words in Lemurian to his niece and nephew, then turns to the passageway.

Stepping outside the stone door, you are blinded by red light streaming from above. For the first time, there are no clouds and you can see the sun. It's impossibly small, but so bright that it stabs at your eye like a dagger.

For the first time you see the inner world as it truly is, the interior of a sphere. The walls of the horizon climb up toward the sky and beyond. Mist, vapor, and dust obscure the other side of the inner world, but you can feel its enormous weight hanging above you.

"Wow, look at this mess!" Peter says. "It's kind of beautiful, though."

You understand what he's talking about. Wherever you look, mud covers all surfaces except the steepest cliffs. Wet streaks mark where it has slipped off. In the valley below, a river of mud burbles at a fast clip. The smell of rich earth reminds you of spring at home.

"Stay on the high ground," Durno warns, leading you along the cliff's edge. "If you fall into one of these sinkholes or pools, it is very hard to get you out. Many have died. As I mentioned when we were planning during the storm, we will follow the trail of the Troglodytes as far as we can, then cross to the main road. Once we get further into Lemurian territory we will be able to travel faster. For now, we walk."

Hours of trudging pass slowly, but eventually Durno calls you to a halt.

"This is a special staircase made by the Troglodytes," he says, motioning to you to enter the gap. "During the Cave Wars over a thousand years ago, the Trogs made sure they had escape routes through their territory and captured lands."

"I thought they didn't like being outside?" Dresdale says.

"They don't," replies Durno. "But they wanted an escape route for emergencies. Before the sun grew brighter, they could tolerate the light of day a bit better. Now, I am not sure they could use this route even in an emergency."

"Still, with the way that they carved through all that stone, why don't they just make escape tunnels?" Dresdale presses.

"They do, Dresdale, they do," Durno says, smiling. "Unfortunately, they have not shared all of their secrets with us. We are ancient enemies after all. Now, let's keep moving."

Entering the staircase, you are amazed by its construction. Carved from the stone, you look up as it spirals toward the top of the cliff.

"I'm *so* glad these stairs aren't covered in mud," Peter says as he trudges behind you. "The treads are so oddly spaced that I think I would break my face in two seconds."

"Me too," you pant, unable to communicate your complete understanding of how alien everything you are encountering truly is.

Once on the top of the cliff, you start to make better time. Durno tells you that you should make it to the main road leading to Light Home, the Lemurian capital, by nightfall. The goal helps you keep going.

You reach a ridgeline, and a wide road in the bottom of a steep valley lies before you. Even from a far distance, you see that there is heavy traffic going in both directions.

"I was starting to think that we were the only ones in this whole place," Peter says. "We haven't seen anything except rocks and mud since we left the Lemurian camp."

"That's not true," Dresdale disagrees. "We saw that fox-like creature earlier today, I think Durno called it an unpance, and there were all sorts of lichens growing in that depression we found on top of the cliff. Some of them were like bushes!"

"Thank you for being so literal, Dres, how silly of me to

forget our two exceptions to the rock and mud scenery," Peter says sourly.

"Come on, guys. We need to keep moving, maybe we should try and make it to the road tonight?" you say, even though your tired legs want to stay at rest.

"It's too dangerous," Durno says. "We'll wait until the bright sun."

You are irritated that everyone just accepts Durno as the leader of your group. He says something and everyone accepts it. Even Dresdale takes his decisions at face value whenever it has to do with logistics. *Maybe I'm just tired, hungry and grumpy,* you think.

Turina and Keldso make camp in a shallow cave, stringing a reddish camouflage tarp across the entrance. They work quickly and wordlessly to get the cooking area prepared and the sleeping pads arranged. Their fluid movements are beautiful as they go about the simple tasks. You are struck again at how different everything is. The weirdest part is that nothing is so strange that it is unrecognizable.

Dinner is dried mushroom slabs with water from a leather skin. Again. It tastes pretty good for a dried mushroom, kind of like beef jerky.

"Don't you have anything else?" Peter whines to Turina.

"No," Turina says with a lilting accent. She and Keldso have picked up a few words of English over the past few days. Dresdale has been learning Lemurian, but the strange words seem to bounce off your brain like water off a stone.

"It's amazing, really. These mushrooms are a completely nutritious diet. I've been talking to Durno about it, and he says that humans as well as Lemurians can survive forever on this stuff, and it's so light that you can carry a month's supply in a small backpack!" Dresdale says as if she had grown them.

"Yay, mushrooms!" Peter says, and you can't help but laugh at the look of disgust on his face.

Durno is keeping a watch tonight. Tired as you are, sleep eludes you.

You nod to him as you slip out of the tent. The sun has dimmed to the point that it is difficult to see color, but you make out objects in this world of half light. Even the reds of the landscape seem to be mere shades of gray.

You navigate the path carefully to the lookout point. Moving down toward the road, you breathe in the coolness of the night air. There are no stars above you. Most of the clouds have drifted to the sides, so all that is giving light is the now dimmed sun. Even dimmed, the sun burns like a bright spark in the sky.

Suddenly, three dark shapes come between you and the sun, casting you briefly into their shadows. The shapes are huge in the sky, and you see great wings beating slowly.

Crouching down to make yourself as unnoticeable as possible, you peer up to see what these flying animals are. The three shapes move out from the ridge and set down on an outcropping of rock only a few hundred feet below you.

Bats. Giant bats. Three dark shapes get off the backs of the huge bats. Metal flashes red in the dim light from the waist of one of the figures. The hood of the one with the glinting metal falls back and you catch sight of his face.

A flash of green light blinds you, and you fall back, dazed.

Sitting back up, you see that the three figures have not reacted to the flash of light and are still busy taking supplies off their mounts. The bats faces are gruesome in the red light. Their folded noses and sharp teeth make them look like moving gargoyles. You look at the figure with the clear face. Once again, you see a wash of green go before your eyes as you see the face of a young man only a few hundred feet away. Your world shifts and you fall into a swirling pool of green light.

The feel of the bat's fur is soft and smells musty, as if you were inside of a cave, instead of out in the open air. Your hands fumble slightly with the clasp of the leather riding harness.

"Move it, Bram," says Morphus in your ear. "We need to have this raid over with before the sun grows bright."

"I know," you say, not really knowing. "I am almost done rigging up the release system."

"You should have done that before, Bram," Morphus hisses. "I thought I trained you better than that? But apparently not. We need to meet with our informer to get the final location of the water processing station. Now you are making me late."

You don't see his hand move, but you feel the sharp blossom of pain from where his dark hand hit the back of your head. Trying to ignore the pain, you focus on setting up the release system. Your momentary clumsiness is gone, and you complete the task quickly.

Looking around, you notice that there is a traveler's shelter above your perch. After meeting the informant, you'll have to go up to clear out any potential witnesses to your presence. Surprise is essential for this mission.

You pull your hood up and follow Morphus and Centurion Afals down the steep path.

You come to not knowing where you are, or who you are. A grinding noise distracts you from your sense of displacement. It's your teeth.

Sitting up, you look down at your hands, and you are relieved that they are the same hands that have always been there, except for a few moments ago, when they were the hands of someone else. Bram, your name had been Bram. *I have to stop them from poisoning the water supply,* you think.

All three figures have left the outcropping. Left behind are the three bats. They have been hobbled, and they hop about the small space awkwardly. You see the three canisters of poison strapped to their chests. The canisters gleam dully in the light. Something has to be done...

Continued on page 1 of The Golden Path
Volume II: Burned By The Inner Sun

ABOUT THE ILLUSTRATOR

Suzanne Nugent received her BFA in illustration from Moore College of Art & Design in Philadelphia, Pennsylvania. She now resides with her husband Fred in Philadelphia and works as a freelance illustrator. She first discovered her love for Choose Your Own Adventure® books when she was only four years old, which inspired her to become an artist.

CREDITS

Many thanks to R. A. Montgomery and Shannon Gilligan for major help with plot, storylines, and editing. Ron Buehl and John Anderson for preliminary ideas and structure. Melissa Bounty for innumerable tasks related to producing the book. John Donoghue for cartography and image help. Nancy Taplin for the beautiful cover illustration, and Dot Greene, Kate Mueller, and Stacey Boyd for book design.

ABOUT THE AUTHOR: ANSON MONTGOMERY

After graduating from Williams College with a degree specialization in ancient history, Anson Montgomery spent ten years founding and working in technology-related companies, as well as working as a reporter for financial and local publications. In the past year he has returned to writing full-time. He is the author of four books in the original Choose Your Own Adventure series, *Everest Adventure, Snowboard Racer, Moon Quest* (reissued in 2008 by Chooseco), and *Cyber Hacker*. With Choose Your Own Adventure® The Golden Path™, he synthesizes his interests and knowledge of ancient civilizations with his passion for science fiction, fantasy, and role-playing. Anson lives and works in Warren, Vermont with his family.